Tarot Haunting

E.B. Sullivan

Tarot Haunting

E.B. Sullivan

"We are not human beings having a spiritual experience. We are spiritual beings having a human experience."
—Pierre Teilhard de Chardin

Prologue
0
The Fool

Cassandra Angelica Visconti, born in a picturesque New England town, grew up in an overprotective home. Her parents showed their love by sheltering her from what they considered a dangerous world.

While the five-letter word worry aptly described her mother, regardless of feeling happy or angry, her father stoically hid his emotions.

From her childhood onward, her parents didn't encourage their only child to voice opinions or question their dogmatic values. Devout in their religious faith, they worked hard and made financial sacrifices in order to send their daughter to Catholic schools.

From as early as Cassandra could remember, everyone called her Cassie. Yet her middle name, Angelica, better described her. A studious child she excelled in her studies. With both parents working, she spent a great deal of time alone. All through grade school and high school, she obeyed her parents by coming directly home from classes. She didn't protest when they told her she couldn't invite friends to their home. Truth was she didn't have many friends. Homely in appearance, taller than her peers, she wore thick lens glasses. Following her mother's instruction Cassie parted her curly hair down the center of her head and make long braids on either side.

On Sundays, donning her plaid school uniform or the unflattering matronly clothes her mother insisted she wear, classmates teased her. During the week, not belonging to any cliques, she didn't linger in the school yard. On warm days, she didn't ride a bike or hang out at the seashore. Rather than risking ridicule, it felt safer to stay in the house completing homework assignments, doing chores, and reading until her mother returned from her office.

Together they prepared dinner.

"Where did you learn to cook?" Cassie asked more than once.

"From your great grandmother, Teresa."

Cassie never tired of hearing her favorite story. "When did that happen?"

"I was nineteen when I married your dad. Days after our wedding, the military deployed him in the Middle East. With the 'Tanker War' going on in the Persian Gulf, I was beside myself with worry. To make matters worse, while he was gone, I discovered I was pregnant. Having a difficult time with morning sickness, I became depressed.

"Your dad's grandmother invited me to live with her. She pretended she was lonely and wanted company. I knew she took pity on me. To get my mind off missing your dad she gave me cooking lessons. A true challenge since I didn't even know how to boil an egg. She was a wonderful Italian cook and generously shared her old world recipes."

As an adolescent, tucked away in the privacy of her room, Cassie enjoyed reading historical novels. Her favorites were set in beautiful castles, palaces, and mansions. Enthralled by the few stories she had heard about her great grandmother, Cassie searched the library for books about Italy's bygone days. From pages describing colorful fictional as well as real personalities, Cassie fabricated daydreams where she was a heroine falling passionately in love with a handsome hero.

In college, she didn't share most young ladies' fascination with fashion and men. Thus, she didn't fit in with her contemporaries. Cassie didn't get caught up with fads. She continued to defer to her mother when shopping for clothes. Certain she'd be rejected, she didn't try out for a sorority. She wasn't asked out on dates or invited to campus parties. She usually spent Saturday nights with good books. She rationalized by telling herself the young men she saw on campus paled in comparison to the dashing supermen she encountered in the stories she read.

After graduating, she attended postgraduate school where she earned a doctor of philosophy degree in history. Through those years, she repeated her isolating pattern.

In contrast to the glamorous females she admired in novels, Cassie's appearance reflected her conservative perspective. Although she purchased her own clothes, they resembled her mother's solid, dark, loose fitting slacks and blouses. Her footwear either black or brown was flat and plain. She continued wearing glasses. She didn't apply make-up to her olive complexion. Frustrated by her coarse, unruly hair she merely pulled it back into a tight bun.

At age twenty-nine, her life was stable and her parents were proud of her. More importantly, they respected Cassie.

She rented a one-bedroom apartment in New York City. To help her set up home, her relatives graciously gave her their discarded furnishings. Although she earned enough money to purchase new items she felt obliged to keep the things other people had given her.

With only a few hours to her parents' home, she frequently spent weekends visiting them.

During the last several years, Cassie established a definite routine: rising at six thirty, showering, drying her hair, dressing, eating a bowl of wheat cereal, and taking the subway to her workplace. Employed by a private research firm, she shared the third floor space with a team of historians. Most often, the area was deafeningly quiet.

Her supervisor, Mrs. Jansen, had an impersonal managing style. She usually communicated via email. Cassie appreciated the precise details provided for each assignment. All day long, sequestered to her tiny cubical she examined articles and prepared reports for university studies, and private individuals needing facts for their nonfiction works.

One morning the phone on Cassie's desk rang. Its shrillness startled her and the other historians.

"Come to my office ASAP," her supervisor requested.

Cassie immediately worried. *Had she messed up in some way?*

She clicked off her computer, briskly walked to the end of the hall, and knocked on Mrs. Jansen's door before entering.

In an atypical, friendly tone, Mrs. Jansen instructed, "Please, take a seat."

Cassie sat on an uncomfortable chair opposite the smiling woman.

"I have a special project for you."

Cassie felt a sense of relief.

"Our client, Mr. Jared Ashbel, the creator of the popular television program *Fact or Truth* is planning an exposé on the occult usurping the true meaning of tarot cards. You'll work closely with him and his staff until he has enough historical data to fill a lengthy segment."

The mention of tarot caused a resurgence of anxiety to churn within Cassie.

Mrs. Jansen continued, "Instead of your regular salary, Mr. Ashbel will be paying you a substantial monthly wage. And at the conclusion of the assignment he intends to give you a sizable bonus."

Regardless of the extra money, Cassie felt she shouldn't delve into tarot. An excuse flew from her lips. "I'm at a critical juncture in the study you gave me two weeks ago. I simply can't take on any more work."

"Send me all your files. I'll complete the report." Mrs. Jansen asked, "Do you know much about tarot?"

Cassie shook her head from side to side thinking, *She knew as a Catholic she shouldn't be interested in it.*

"Mr. Ashbel specifically requested you," Mrs. Jansen shrugged her shoulders, "but he wouldn't disclose why."

Like a tug of war, two sides of Cassie pulled to gain dominance. One side warned she should refuse the assignment even if it meant losing her position. The other side promised the task would be a stimulating adventure.

She listened to Mrs. Jansen, "Mr. Ashbel is an important client. He's a man I wouldn't dream of disappointing. I suggest you spend the rest of the day doing a little background work before you report to the television station tomorrow."

She handed Cassie an envelope. "You'll find the details of where, when, and whom to report to in here."

With mixed emotions and shaky hands, Cassie returned to her desk. While she uploaded the files of her present assignment and emailed them to her supervisor, Cassie recalled, the day of her job interview.

Her first time in New York City, she arrived three hours early for her appointment. While waiting, she decided to wander through the exhibition halls of the nearby Morgan Library and Museum. Too nervous to pay attention to most displays she suddenly froze. Her eyes fixed on the Visconti-Sforza tarot cards. Their brilliantly painted images survived from the fifteenth century.

She quickly learned they originated in Milan, Italy and comprised one of the oldest tarot card decks. Absorbed in her discovery, Cassie lost track of time. When she glanced at her watch, she dashed out of the museum, ran through the streets, entered the tall building, and took the elevator to her destination.

Minutes later, a panel of experts drilled her on research strategies and statistical paradigms.

Once the grueling interview was over, rather than thinking about her responses, her mind drifted to the tarot cards she had viewed earlier. She wondered, *Why hadn't someone in her family mentioned them?*

Cassie stopped at a cafe, ordered coffee, and called her parents' home.

Her mother immediately asked, "How'd the interview go?"

"I won't know for a couple of days."

"I'm sure you did well."

"Thanks for your confidence. Hope you're right."

"What do you think of the big city?"

"It's an amazing place filled with surprises." Cassie described her trip to the museum and asked, "Mom, did you ever hear of the Visconti-Sforza tarot cards?"

"Don't even look at them. Tarot cards are evil."

"They were originally made in the 1440s for the Duke of Milan's court."

Her mother's voice was firm and definite, "The Catholic Church forbids us to believe in divining or any form of fortunetelling."

"The cards weren't intended for those purposes. Although classified as playing cards it's believed they were designed as an enlightening experience for pilgrims seeking spiritual understanding."

Her mother pleaded, "Promise you'll forget the cards."

Cassie knew it wise to reply, "Sure, Mom."

Once she moved to New York City, Cassie revisited the Morgan Library and Museum. At the gift shop, she purchased a duplicate deck of the Visconti tarot cards. That night she admired the exquisite illustrations painted by famous Renaissance artists. On the Major Arcana or triumphs, numbered zero through twenty-one, she noticed visual references to Visconti family traditions.

Cassie's heart pounded. She longed to understand the many symbols contained on each card.

A feeling of guilt washed over her. She put the cards back in their box. She placed the box on the top shelf of her coat closet.

Wanting to obey her mother, Cassie tried to forget them.

Despite her attempts, tarot seemed to haunt her.

Ads popped up in newspapers and magazines advertising fortunetellers who read tarot cards.

On a street near her apartment, neon lights flashed *Tarot Readings*.

In the break room, a group of coworkers asked Cassie to join them. "We're having a tarot party and invited a card romancer. She does incredible readings." Without giving a reason, Cassie declined the invitation.

On many a night, Cassie dreamed of the complex images colorfully adorning the twenty-two Major Arcana. She often wondered how the occult derailed the tarot from its holy path and placed tarot down a dark road.

She jokingly referred to her assorted thoughts as personal dialogues with tarot's ghost. She felt a calling from this mythical spirit to vindicate the cards and eradicate the decks' tarnished reputation.

With her present assignment of researching the mysterious decks, Cassie felt an uncanny exhilaration. Because of her Visconti heritage, she felt destined to uncover the truth about tarot. She also, felt a longing to embrace researching the decks in order to proclaim their original intentions.

She read various interpretations of the cards. Most commentators agreed, their symbols transcend ordinary realities and offer a connection to another dimension. Religious scholars pointed to biblical revelations. Some claimed the cards provide a pathway straight to God.

From a psychological perspective, individual interpretations could focus on a few of the multiple symbols to illuminate inner conflicts.

Jungian interpretations explained the cards as brain pictures drawn from the collective unconscious and representing archetypical figures.

She reviewed several decks. The most popular was the Rider-Waite tarot deck. She read The Church of Yahweh's website. With an emphasis on Christian imagery, it contained detailed and fascinating interpretations of these particular cards. Ironically, by the time Arthur Edward Waite had illustrator Pamela Colman Smith copy the images, the cards had taken on a fortunetelling mystique.

Cassie scanned and saved each card in a file.

She couldn't imagine why Jared Ashbel, the famous television personality, hired anyone to provide tarot information. The internet contained scores of articles, books, blogs, and websites filled with interpretive materials and artistic commentaries regarding the many decks.

She laughed at how people misused tarot in silly ways from illustrating them with Disney characters to the devil. Again, she wondered how the misguided use of the cards, namely fortunetelling, was popularly associated with the original decks.

In her mind, she asked her tarot's phantom ghost, *Did the occult innocently borrow the concept of the cards, merely because they were available? Hundreds of years after the cards' creation, did the occult intentionally steal tarot and wage a campaign to defame the original intent of the cards, cloud their holy symbols, and distort the value of the cards?*

She thought of something she first learned in grammar school and relearned many times since, God created only good.

In general, evil didn't create anything. Rather, it took what was good and transformed it into negativity.

Cassie felt the occult's transformed decks were a malevolent mockery of the original and almost sacred tarot cards.

She scribbled notes. She felt comfortable doing her job of compiling data. Like other assignments, Cassie didn't have to agree or disagree with information. All she had to do was research other people's opinions.

This assignment felt different. Emotions flooded her. She needed to separate her feelings, her beliefs, from objective research.

Cassie studied an image of the first Major Arcana. It was numbered zero and named the Fool.

One theological interpretation explained the card captures the moment of silence before God created the universe.

The card symbolized endless possibilities.

She chuckled. The card seemed to predict her situation. At this stage, she had no idea where her upcoming assignment would lead.

Mrs. Jansen stopped by Cassie's desk. "Best you leave for the day. I wouldn't want you tuckered out when you report to the folks at the television station."

Cassie didn't hesitate to follow her supervisor's suggestion.

Upon entering her apartment, Cassie opened her coat closet and reached up for her deck of the Visconti-Sforza tarot cards. Using Roman numerals instead of Hebrew ones, these cards had nothing to do with Kabbalah, Jewish mysticism.

She sat at the mahogany dining room table. It had belonged to her great grandmother, Teresa. She stroked the distinctive grain and envisioned its surface covered with delicious food.

She removed the card labeled 0, The Fool. She studied it and wondered, Are *the seven pens in his hair a reference to the seven days it took the Lord to create the universe?*

She read about the Fool standing on the edge of a cliff. It could represent someone apart from the community, someone a bit mad.

She held the card over her heart, closed her eyes, and thought.

Was she stepping off the edge of her trouble free world?

Was she about to betray her religious foundation?

Was she committing to a trickster's venture?

Was she a fool detouring from establishment's religious roots?

Regardless of her questions, she felt determined to conduct a methodical investigation. She felt ready to take the first step and commit to a questionable journey.

She walked across the room and stared into an antique beveled mirror over the fireplace. Her great aunt Josephine had given it to her. Cassie cherished the heirloom. She wondered about the many faces that peered into the reflecting glass. *Had other relatives taken unnecessary risks or had they conservatively lived pragmatic lives?*

As she peered at her image, she thought about the origin of her name.

Greek mythology introduces Cassandra as the daughter of Trojan King Priam and Queen Hecuba. Legend claims Apollo felt attracted to Cassandra's beauty. In order to seduce her he gave her the gift of prophecy. When she refused to be intimate with him, he felt cheated, angry, and vengeful. Spewing forth his rage, he placed a curse on Cassandra. Although her prophecies were true, no one believed them. Instead, many people considered Cassandra insane.

Like the pictured mythical Cassandra, Cassie also had dark brown, curly hair and brown eyes. She wondered if she too was crazy.

She told herself, "Maybe I'm a fool, because I've decided to commit to an undefined challenge. Maybe I'm mad, because I'm ready to jump off a predictable existence into an unknown life changing spiritual journey."

She wondered, *Maybe even if her findings were true, no one would believe them.*

A burning excitement convinced her to delve heart, mind, and soul into this venture.

She mused, *Just maybe she was called to be what her other Greek name, Angelica implies: a messenger of God.*

Chapter One
I
The Magician

Next morning when Cassie left her comfortable, air-conditioned apartment, hot, muggy air assaulted her. Gray clouds loomed overhead. As she walked three short blocks to the subway station, she imagined her smoothly combed hair beginning to frizz. She was glad she had confined most of her curly locks in a tight bun.

Traveling uptown rather than to her midtown office, she was surprised at the crowded platform. People pressed and pushed her forward into the car. In the frenzied boarding process, the pins holding her hair in place came loose and fell. Pressed up against strangers it was impossible for Cassie to bend down and search for them.

Eleven stops later, she exited the station.

People dressed in business attire filled the streets.

Horns honked, but the traffic hardly moved.

One, two, three raindrops splashed her face before a downpour drenched her.

Soaking wet she arrived at the television station's tall office building. She removed her glasses, pulled out a tissue from her purse and dried them. When she put her glasses back on, she saw white specks clinging to the lenses.

A receptionist sitting at an information desk asked, "Can I help you?"

"I have an appointment with Mr. Ashbel."

"Your name?"

"Cassie."

The woman stared at her.

"Cassie Visconti."

"Just a moment, please, while I check his schedule."

Cassie realized she must look a fright with dripping hair and wet clothes.

"Dr. Visconti, I see you're expected. Take the far elevator to the twenty-second floor. I'll let Mr. Ashbel know you're on your way."

Cassie wished she had time to tidy up before meeting the client, but the receptionist was already speaking on the phone, "Mr. Ashbel's nine o'clock arrived."

Despite her disheveled appearance, Cassie felt prepared for her meeting with the network personality. In her briefcase was a folder filled with an organized timeline of tarot's history.

Picture cards dating to ancient Egyptian times may have influenced twelfth century rabbis. Facing religious oppression and fearing Muslims and Christians would destroy Jewish culture these men recorded their sacred teachings by imbedding them in cryptic symbolic illustrations.

Since there are twenty-two Major Arcana in a tarot deck, during the express elevator ride to the twenty-second floor, Cassie wondered, like the twenty-two letters of the Hebrew alphabet and the twenty-two chapters of St. John's book of Revelation, was this a mere coincidence or a significant omen.

Sooner than expected the elevator stopped. When the doors opened, a stunning, statuesque woman introduced herself.

"Hi. I'm Crystal. Mr. Ashbel asked me to greet you."

Cassie stepped into the hallway.

Crystal extended her right hand. With a firm grip, she shook Cassie's hand.

"Unfortunately Jared had to leave the city. He'd like us to work together in preparing a brief intro, something of a commercial for the tarot segment."

"But..."

"Don't worry. We'll fix you up long before taking any photos."

They walked past several offices before entering one.

"First stop." Crystal introduced Cassie to Dr. Franz. "He's our staff optometrist."

A man wearing a white coat smiled at a bewildered Cassie and explained, "The network doesn't like too many of their stars wearing glasses. With your permission I'd like to fit you for contact lenses."

"I've had poor eyesight for as long as I can remember. I'd hate to waste your time. I don't think I'm a good candidate for contacts."

He gave her a reassuring pat on her shoulder and escorted Cassie into a smaller room where he proceeded to examine her eyes.

Obedient Cassie didn't object. She patiently participated in the examination and tests.

After his exam he stated, "Since you're both nearsighted and farsighted, I recommend you wear mono lenses."

"I'm not familiar with the term."

"One lens will correct your vision for close up work. The other will enable you to see at a distance. Your brain will adjust to using the appropriate eye as your focus changes from viewing things close up when reading to a distance while walking."

Before placing soft lenses into her eyes, Dr. Frantz asked, "May I?"

She nodded.

A minute later, Cassie exclaimed, "I can't believe I can see without glasses."

"Get up slowly."

She stood.

"Do you feel dizzy?"

"No. No. I feel… liberated."

He had her practice inserting and removing lenses.

"You can wear these for two weeks, day and night, before disposing them." He handed her a small box. "I've given you an extra trial pair. Any problems call me or stop by. If these work out for you I'll send you a six month supply of contracts."

She slipped the box in her purse and vigorously shook his hand. "I can't thank you enough. How much do I owe you?"

He laughed. "My dear, the network pays for my services."

Crystal was waiting in the reception room. She led Cassie down the hall through a set of double doors.

Cassie stared at a large space. Stations resembling those in a beauty salon lined an entire wall. Opposite were dressing rooms. In between were platforms. A gray haired gentleman was standing on one. A tailor was chalking his suit jacket.

Crystal's cheery voice piped up, "Voilá. This is the place where the real magic happens."

A man with spiked blond hair, wearing diamond studded earrings and a black smock came up to them. He winked at Crystal and shook Cassie's hand.

"I'm Tomas, your stylist and makeup artist." He pointed toward a dressing room. "Go get comfy, sweetie."

Crystal walked with Cassie and followed her into one of the booths. "Before you change I'll get your vital statistics." She unrolled a yellow tape and quickly measured Cassie in several places. "Pretty darn nice. How tall are you?"

"Five-seven."

And what's your shoe size?"

"Eight."

Crystal waved. "See you later."

Within the changing room, feeling perplexed, Cassie shed her damp clothes, donned a white terrycloth robe, and slipped her feet into matching slippers. Carrying her briefcase and purse, she opened the room's door.

Tomas was waiting. "You can leave your things here. They'll be safe."

Cassie obeyed and followed Tomas.

"We'll start with a shampoo."

"I don't understand."

"Just standard procedure."

Tomas took his time. He added a special conditioner and placed a plastic bag on Cassie's head. "While you're under the dryer for a few would you like coffee or tea?"

"No thanks."

"How about a muffin or a bagel to nosh?"

"Thank you, but I had breakfast at home."

He handed her a stack of magazines. "Happy reading, sweetie."

Twenty minutes later, he returned. He rinsed her hair and combed out tangles. "What a wonderful head of hair you have. Other than a few strategic cuts I think it'll be perfect for your upcoming role."

He measured strands on the right and left sides of her head making snips here and there. Cassie watched as wavy tresses fell to the floor.

His fingertips weaved an oily product through her curls before blow-drying them with a diffusing attachment.

He fluffed her ends with a large, round brush and sprayed a citrus mist over her entire head.

"That was easy."

She stared at her image. Although she liked the look, she worried. "I can't wear my hair down. In no time, it'll turn into a frizzy mess."

Tomas ignored her comment. "Now for the fun part."

He held her shoulders and studied her face. "Your eyes are an exceedingly rich chocolate brown."

"I've always considered them... ordinary."

"Not in the least. A man could easily get deliciously lost in them."

Tomas opened a case containing an organized display of various sized jars, tubes, and tins.

Cassie felt awkward. Other than occasionally wearing a subtle shade of lip-gloss, unlike other young women, she had no interest in makeup.

Tomas applied two different creams to her face. "You have soft, flawless skin, no sun damage, and no freckles."

"Working inside may have helped."

He turned Cassie away from the mirror before scrutinized his supplies.

Cassie recalled the day of a school Halloween parade. In a rare playful moment, her mother decorated Cassie's face. When she looked in the mirror, despite wearing a ballerina costume, with red circles on her cheeks, exaggerated lips, and arched brows, she felt like a clown.

Tomas placed one finger under her chin. "Close your eyes."

With a gentle touch, he applied shadow, liner, and mascara,

She asked, "Do you like this part of your job?"

"No. I love it. Every face is like a blank canvas offering possibilities awaiting discovery." He dotted her face with a silky liquid.

With each pat, Cassie felt his creative energy.

"I think a bronzer will make your high cheek bones even more prominent." He brushed the sides of her face.

Lastly, Tomas applied lip color. He gave Cassie a hand mirror "What do you think?"

Before Cassie could comment, Crystal came into the room and twirled Cassie's chair around.

"Great work. Tomas, you've captured the image Jared was after. I'll just take a few photos for him." She raised her iPad and snapped away.

Crystal addressed Cassie. "Looks like you're ready for a fitting." She led Cassie to a dressing room where a tall attractive woman was standing. "This is Margo. She'll assist you."

Margo shook Cassie's hand. "I'll hang several undergarments over the door. Try them on. When you find something that feels right give me a holler."

Cassie took off the robe and stepped out of the slippers. As she tried on lacy foundations, she felt like her body was evolving from a budding teenager into a voluptuous woman.

Without the aid of a mirror, she relied on her sensations. In contrast to the practical foundations she usually wore, the silky fabrics felt luxurious against her skin.

"Can I come in?" Without waiting for a reply, Margo carrying a garment bag joined Cassie in the confined space. She hung up the bag.

"I'll just make a few adjustments." She hooked Cassie's bra to the tightest point and raised its straps.

As Cassie felt her breasts overflowing from the top of the cream-colored material she sensed God had given her more feminine attributes than she realized.

Margo unzipped the garment bag. "Get into these. I'll be right outside," she said before leaving Cassie alone.

A few minutes later, Cassie opened the door. In stocking feet, due to the tightness of her skirt, she took tiny steps climbing to Margo who stood on the top of a round platform.

Since the outfit felt snug, Cassie expected Margo to let out a few seams. Instead, she began tucking, pinning, and stitching.

With each tug, Cassie felt her anxiety level rising. Her mother would emphatically disapprove of this outfit.

Cassie closed her eyes. To calm her nerves she thought of something she learned while researching tarot. In the Hebrew language God's real name, Ahyh, means, I will be what I will be.

Was this a message for each of us?

Cassie wanted to be what she would be.

Margo's voice interrupted her. "Please step into these."

Cassie looked down at a pair of suede, aqua, three-inch heels.

When her feet slipped into them, she felt a kinship with Cinderella on the night of the royal ball.

Margo instructed, "Stay right there. I'll just be a moment."

Cassie watched Margo half expecting the woman, like a fairy godmother, to return with a magic wand.

Margo wheeled a folded screen to the base of the platform. She opened the panels revealing three full-length mirrors.

Cassie peered at someone she hardly recognized. The pale blue, straight, short skirt had two side slits. The tight, collarless, sweater with its plunged neckline showed more than a hint of cleavage.

She blushed.

Crystal entered the room and snapped a few more photos. "Tomas and Margo, thanks for jobs well done."

As the pair was leaving the room, Cassie echoed, "Thank you." They disappeared before she could tell them she perceived them as miracle workers.

In the next instant, she questioned, *Were Tomas and Margo artists or charlatans?*

Cassie hoped the results of her magicians' work would guide her to enhance rather than exploit upcoming opportunities.

She chided herself. After all, television programs provided entertainment. Audiences were aware actors performed fictional roles.

Crystal asked, "Is there anything at your place needing attention like a dog, cat, or lover?"

"No. I live alone."

"Just wanted to check. While you're assisting Jared, he's made arrangements for you to stay at the Plaza. A car and driver will be at your disposal to take you around town. Margo will stock your closets with an initial wardrobe. She'll be on call to accompany you to a host of boutiques carrying designer fashions and accessories. Freely purchase additional items and charge whatever you wish to the network. Tomas will pop up to your room each morning to style your hair and apply makeup. Of course he'll be available for touchups during the day and evenings when necessary.

"Next stop is the personnel office. You'll need to get acquainted with network policies and fill out insurance and other standard forms."

Cassie felt her head spin. "What about my research?"

"If Jared is satisfied with your head shots, a graphic designer will set up your website."

"My website?"

"And of course, in order for you to send and receive information, the tech will establish your official email address."

"I already have an email address."

"Anyone as sexy as you needs a seductive name. From now, you can post your findings in a blog on www.Dr.CassandraAngelicaVisconti.com."

Although she felt she was a temporary guest in another person's body, for the moment, Cassie thought her real name suited her new image.

Chapter Two

II
The High Priestess

While walking up the red-carpeted steps of the Plaza Hotel, not used to wearing high heels, Cassandra's ankle buckled. Pausing to gain her footing, she gazed at the stained glass window above the entryway. She studied its exquisite design before taking a few steps forward.

A uniformed man held open the door of New York City's century-old landmark.

Carrying her purse and briefcase, she stepped into the fabulous lobby. Marbled floors under her feet, coffered ceiling above her head, and massive crystal chandeliers lit her way.

Feeling like a little girl playing dress up, she moved ever so slowly.

The manager greeted her at the registration desk. "Dr. Visconti, your belongings have arrived, and hopefully organized to your liking. Let us know if we can be of any additional assistance."

Playing the part, she signed the register using an exaggerated flare of curlicues.

"The bellhop will show you to the Carnegie Park Suite on the nineteenth floor."

She followed yet another uniformed man to the elevator. After he pressed buttons, she stated, "Glad it stopped raining."

"Yes ma'am."

When he led her into the suite, Cassandra studied the understated classy parlor with its gray tufted couch, modern design area rug, two yellow upholstered chairs, and an antique French writing desk.

She felt drawn to the window.

"Central Park, I presume?"

He nodded. "Looks like you have a message." He pointed to the telephone's blinking light.

"Thank you." She attempted to give him a tip, but he refused to accept one.

"The network takes good care of us, ma'am."

As she picked up the receiver, he discreetly made his exit.

She heard a masculine voice identify himself as Jared Ashbel. "Please meet me at the Plaza's Champagne Bar this evening at 7:00. No need to reply unless you can't keep our date."

Although she knew this would be a business meeting, Cassandra felt thrilled to have a 'date' with a celebrity.

In the next moment, she felt anxious. She wondered, *What should she wear to such a fancy establishment?*

She remembered something about Margo providing an initial wardrobe.

Cassandra went into the bedroom. Muted beige tones welcomed her. She opened the wood-paneled closet doors. Colorful, casual to formal clothes hung on satin hangers. She opened built-in drawers containing delicate undergarments and sexy negligees.

She felt overwhelmed.

Then she glanced at the bed. A deep purple sheath stood out on the ivory bedspread. When she walked closer, she almost tripped over a hot pink pair of pointed toed high heels. Amethyst studded earrings were on the night table. Peeking from underneath the silk dress were lavender undergarments trimmed with pink ribbons.

She stepped onto the bathroom's mosaic floor. Walls decorated with a gilded floral motif provided a charming backdrop for a pedestal sink, soaking tub, and separate shower all fitted with gold faucets.

She took off her clothes, folded them, and neatly put them aside. She turned on the water taps, stuffed her hair into a shower cap, stepped in the tub, and poured liquid from a curved bottle. She slithered under the white foamy wetness.

In the soothing environment, she felt bewildered.

Magicians Tomas and Margo had created her image but it was up to Cassandra to give birth to her new character.

How could she fit into her role?

She had the appearance of a sophisticated woman but the mentality of a timid recluse. Once she opened her mouth, dowdy Cassie would erase magical Cassandra.

She closed her eyes and prayed for guidance.

Images of strong, confident, and authentic heroines paraded in her mind.

Regardless of historical settings, Cassandra identified with the personalities she came to know through written words.

She stepped out of the tub.

An answer to her dilemma occurred to her. *All she had to do was reflect the classic essence of any of these women.*

But how?

As she wrapped a fluffy towel around her body, another thought popped into her head. *Like everyone else, she contained the elements of earth, water, air, and fire.*

Tomas and Margo reinvented the solid or earth part of this equation. They had commented Cassandra's natural physical attributes made their work easy. She knew differently. They were magicians.

Cassandra applied a sweet smelling body lotion, removed the shower cap, and tossed her curls. She checked her makeup. It was ruined. She glanced at the marble vanity countertop at additional supplies including some makeup. After washing her face, she applied a face cream and trying to put into practice tricks Tomas had taught her, she subtly decorated her face.

She reassured herself, later this evening, just as she had done while walking into the hotel, she could playact.

Dressing in sexy undergarments and slithering into the tight fitting dress she thought, *As water adapts to whatever shape container it fills, she could adjust to the shape of her new role.*

Peering in the full-length mirror her first sensation was to blush. She felt embarrassed. Her dress showed her curves, her long legs, and much of her voluptuous cleavage.

But the more she stared at her image the more she liked it.

The reflection from a lit lamp created a halo effect causing Cassandra to smile.

She went to the living room's writing desk. She spread out the Visconti tarot cards and studied the first three Major Arcana. She remembered reading the Fool was androgynous. The Magician was male, and the card labeled II, the High Priestess, was female.

Together the three cards created a trinity. It was different than the Holy Trinity where the Father, Son and Holy Spirit are 'one God in three Divine Persons.' It was different than the Holy Family consisting of the love shared by Joseph, Mary, and Jesus.

Yet, the three cards had a definite relationship. The first card suggested the possibility to create. The second presented opportunities to manipulate creations. The third card offered the energy to animate the creation.

Cassandra held up the third Arcana, the High Priestess card. Wearing a triple crown, she carried a cross in one hand and a book in the other.

Cassandra, like the depicted image, had deep faith and trusted God was always at her side ready to be her guide.

Familiar fictional and nonfictional characters revisited her thoughts. The female protagonists embodied traits which prevented them from straying from noble paths.

Although she would never be mistaken as a heroine, Cassandra had heroic core beliefs.

She left the cards and, again, stood in front of the full-length mirror.

She practiced moving her arms, walking, and swaying until she felt her movements were as fluid as water.

Could she make her imaged persona a reality?

She took in deep breaths allowing the air she breathed to calm her rattled nerves.

With over an hour to spare before meeting Mr. Ashbel, she needed to contain her frazzled nerves. She tried to quell her anxiety by telling herself she didn't need to pretend. She only needed to show him her inner-self.

She left the room and took the elevator to the hotel's shops.

She felt a strong urge to send her mother a gift.

She peeked at the spectacular pieces in Maurice Fine Jewelry store and moved on. She skipped Assouline Books and Gifts, because she knew she could easily spend too much time browsing their collection.

Asulin Galleries offered exquisite antiques.

She stepped in Gramercy Flowers.

"Can I help you?" a friendly voice asked.

"I'd like to send my mother a surprise."

"Any special occasion?"

The truth resounded in her mind, *Atonement for her guilt.*

Cassandra knew her mother would condemn her tarot research. She also suspected her mother wouldn't approve of Cassandra's short, tight fitting dress with its provocative neckline. And, she could add role-playing as another reason for feeling guilty.

She replied, "I just want to remind her how much I love her."

In the process of choosing just the right flowers, Cassandra learned the flower shop, established in 1904, was New York City's oldest family owned and operated floral business.

She also noticed the woman seemed upset.

"Are you okay?" Cassandra asked.

"It's that obvious. I'm sorry. I should learn to hide my emotions especially while working."

Cassandra forgot all about trying to act sophisticated or intelligent. She suggested, "Maybe it'll help to talk about it."

The woman shared, "I'm confused about this guy. He's great looking, considerate, and most times fun to be around."

"But?"

"But… I don't want to sound like a snob, but he's different than anyone I usually hang with."

"Different how?"

"Don't get me wrong. I'm no angel. But, a few things about him bother me. His idea of a dream vacation is spending a week in Las Vegas gambling. He often uses crude language. He refuses to go to dinner with me at my folks' place and he's adamant about never having children."

Feeling an inspiration, like a flame burning within her, Cassandra who typically didn't voice her opinions surprised herself by asking a personal question. "Why are you with him?"

"Like I said he's fun."

"Are you hoping he'll change?"

"The thought has crossed my mind."

"How long have you two been dating?"

"Over a year and I'm sure he's about to ask the big question."

Cassandra looked at the stylishly dressed, attractive woman. "Although I have no right to give advice I can't help but notice your good fashion sense."

"Coming from a woman as elegant as you I consider your words quite a compliment."

Cassandra felt yet another pang of guilt. Her usual attire reflected she didn't know anything about latest styles. She pushed her feelings aside and said, "Imagine seeing a wonderful outfit in your favorite shop."

"That's easy. It would be the one I saw the other day, the one I can't afford."

"Let's pretend it's on a super sale. You rush to try it on and look in the mirror. The outfit is baggy where it should be form fitting." Cassandra thought of one of her outfits. "It flattens your chest and the color makes your face look ashen."

"Yuck."

"Would you buy it just because you like it? Would you buy it because you can afford it? Despite how poorly it fit, if you owned it, would you wear it?" She didn't say, *would you feel comfortable in it because your mother approved of it?*

The woman emphatically said, "Absolutely not."

"Why not?"

"Because it doesn't fit me. Even though it's pretty it isn't right for me." Her face lit up. "Wait a minute. I get it. My boyfriend is like the lovely outfit. He's handsome and fun at times, but he doesn't suit me."

Cassandra nodded. "What time is it?"

"Six-fifty, and definitely time to drop the guy."

"Sorry, but I have a seven o'clock appointment with my new boss."

The woman patted Cassandra's arm. "I can't tell you how much better I feel." She asked, "Are you a guest of the hotel?"

"Yes."

"I'll just charge the flowers to your room. They'll be delivered by noon tomorrow."

Cassandra wouldn't dream of having the television station pay for her mother's gift.

She gave the woman her credit card. "No thank you. I'd prefer to pay for them now."

After the transaction was complete, the woman hugged Cassandra. "I can't believe within a few minutes you helped shed a new light on my love life. Rather than grieving what I'll lose I'm ready to focus on what I gained—an opportunity to find a guy who does fit me."

Cassandra smiled warmly before dashing out of the shop.

As she made her way toward the bar, she assessed her day. Earlier she willingly participated in what she considered a form of deceit. She allowed professional conjurers Crystal, Dr. Franz, Tomas, and Margo give her a magical new image.

Yet, in the flower shop, with her make-believe glamorous appearance, Cassandra behaved as she always wished she could and attempted to help someone.

Throughout her school years, she overheard classmates in distress. Perhaps, many exaggerated their plights, were overdramatic, and selfish. Nevertheless, she seemed to have logical solutions. She longed to share analogies with them to help them see how easy it was to problem-solve.

More recently, at her office, she heard colleagues whisper about their personal dilemmas. Without making judgments or giving direct advice, she thought of analogies that might help distressed coworkers gain broader perspectives. However, feeling insecure, she didn't share her thoughts.

This was the first time Cassandra directly interacted. This was the first time she had the courage to share her insights. From the florist's comments, Cassandra felt reassured.

Soon, her real test would begin. She was aware she had the freedom to act correctly or incorrectly to influence her destiny. Regardless of Mr. Jared Ashbel's possible temptations, in everything she did, it was Cassandra's responsibility, like tarot's High Priestess, to stay within the narrow corridor between abundant blessings and good judgment.

She took a deep breath before entering the Champagne Bar.

Surrounded by the splendid ambiance Cassandra was ready to tell her boss what she had discovered even if it meant she'd have to leave the opulent hotel and return to her tiny work cubicle.

Chapter Three

III
The Empress

Cassandra walked through the doors of the Plaza Hotel's Champagne Bar and felt as if she had stepped back to the early 1900s. She craned her neck peering into the smartly decorated space. She half expected to see women wearing long flowing dresses and men donned in pinstriped suits.

She took a few steps forward and locked eyes with a man moving toward her. Not exactly handsome, yet, he conveyed a magnetic presence.

His deep-set dark eyes held hers in their gaze.

As if mesmerized, she stood perfectly still and waited until he reached her.

He lifted her hands and gave them a slight squeeze. "Hi Cassandra. I'm Jared."

A hot current shot through her. The sensation disarmed her.

"Hello," she managed.

Following him to a round table flanked with two green, velvet Victorian chairs she noticed his gray streaked hair complemented his light gray shirt and dark gray slacks.

"I've taken the liberty of ordering champagne or would you prefer something else?"

The sound of his masculine voice made her heartbeat race. Feeling a bit out of breath, Cassandra reminded herself he wasn't a romantic character from a novel. He was only a man. And more importantly, he was her employer.

The wine steward turned the label in Jared's direction and said, "1990 Veuve Clicquot Brut." He gave

Jared time to peruse the bottle before pouring the bubbly libation into two champagne flutes.

"Thank you," Jared respectfully replied.

A waiter placed a platter of hummus, cucumber, and pita on the small table.

Cassandra told him, "Good choice. I love hummus."

Jared raised his glass, "Let's toast to our joint venture."

She lifted her glass.

Their delicate stemware clinked.

She took a short sip followed by a longer one.

He asked, "Do you like it?"

"I usually find champagne too sweet, but this is…well for the first time I understood why people adore it."

He chuckled.

Having revealed her lack of worldliness, she felt foolish.

She stared at him thinking Jared seemed her opposite. Of course, as male and female they automatically represented duality. But there were other differences. He personified the stereotypic suave, sophisticated, society type while she was a bumbling, naïve, small town girl.

Before she made other childish statements or lost her courage, she focused on what she had to tell him. She recited her prepared script, "I don't think you need my services. Scores of articles and books explain the roots and evolution of tarot. I don't understand why you contacted my firm and specifically requested me."

"I chose you to research tarot, because you're an historian. You're a professional who can synthesize data and present it succinctly. Your educated prospective will undoubtedly elucidate germane facts and speculative theories. But quite frankly, I handpicked you for this position because of who you are."

She tilted her head, "Now I'm really puzzled."

"You're Cassandra Angelica Visconti a direct descendant of Maria Fillipo Visconti, Duke of Milan. Didn't the first tarot deck originate in his court?"

"Yes. However, Visconti family members didn't pass down secrets from the fifteen century to the present. At least, not in my family."

"Of course not, but your heritage brings a certain," he waved one hand through the air, "theatrical touch to my production."

"Oh. I see. You'd like my name to be listed in the show's credits."

"Not just that. I see you as an essential part of the production."

"How so?"

"Your research will go to our script department. You'll give staff-writers direction. You'll edit their work making sure it conveys your viewpoints. And I want you to be my cohost."

Cassandra felt a sudden, cold chill ripple through her body. Her arms crossed her chest. Her hands gripped her shoulders. A list of reasons to decline this assignment swirled in her mind.

She couldn't appear on national television.

She hated making public speeches.

She suffered from stage fright.

And her mother would learn about Cassandra's involvement with tarot.

She told him, "I don't know the first thing about acting."

"I beg to disagree."

Was he alluding to her role-playing? Could he tell she was pretending to be a fictitious character from a romance novel?

His words evaporated her thoughts. "You're beautiful, intelligent, and, in my opinion, simply perfect to narrate the segment."

She felt her cheeks burn. To deflect his compliments she returned to defending her statement about him not needing her services. "I don't even think the occult's use of tarot needs debunking. It's a known fact tarot's original purpose had nothing to do with fortunetelling."

"Remember the name of my show is *Fact or Truth*. Most folks don't know the facts or the truth about tarot. Majority believe tarot cards are synonymous with the occult. They see the decks as instruments of some sort of witchcraft.

"Ask any person on the street. The mere mention of tarot conjures up visions of the devil.

"In short, ordinary people fear tarot."

Cassandra knew her mother fit in the terrorized by tarot category.

He continued, "Fear stops most people from investigating the cards. They believe in the fiction surrounding the decks. They don't want to learn facts and they certainly don't seek the truth. While a few hold tarot in mystical esteem, far fewer folks realize it's been corrupted."

He paused until her eyes met his intense stare. "I want you to tell the average Joe and Jane the truth. I want you to expose the myth. Our television special will dispel illusions. Like a good teacher it will stimulate secular and religious truth seekers."

Cassandra felt compelled to respond. "Theologians studied the truth about tarot. Did you know, Monk Valentin Tomberg's *Meditations on the Tarot* was seen on canonized Pope John Paul II's desk?"

Trying to reinforce her point, she didn't wait for him to reply. "Even the name of the deck illustrates its meaning."

She opened her small purse and retrieved a pen. She printed letters on a paper cocktail napkin and turned the napkin toward Jared.

T

A   O

R

Starting from the top, she pointed to the letters in one direction. "These read?"

He answered, "TARO."

"Tarot, the subject of our discussion."

Starting from the top, she pointed to the letters in the other direction. "These read?"

"TORA."

"The torah means instruction. It offers a way of life to those who choose to follow it. It's the central reference of the Judaic tradition and contains the first five books of the twenty-four books of the Tanakh.

Starting from the bottom, she pointed to the letters in one direction. "These read?"

"ROTA."

"Rota is the Latin word for wheel. Thus, the Torah leads to tarot and tarot leads to the Torah."

Jared stood, walked over to her side of the table, bent over, and kissed each of her cheeks. "You're fabulous especially when fired up. I guessed you were perfect for this job. Now I'm convinced you'll be the one to set the record straight."

He lowered his body and leaned close to her face. "I want you to provide people with the beauty of tarot's art and explain messages from its biblical origins, from the Old and New Testaments, from Judaism and Christianity."

"Why don't you present the facts?"

"Because my role is to debate everything you say."

Although she thought his shows focused on sensationalism, she thought in this case his approach made sense.

He kept talking. "I know my audience. I've successfully presented debunking segments for several years. My strategy is to whet discerning folks' appetites. One show has the potential to encourage millions of people to seek knowledge. "

The more he spoke, the more she felt seduced by his intellectual motivation. Still she didn't want to be seen on his show. "I don't doubt you have your hands on the pulse of our modern day culture, but I'm not the right person to…"

His authoritative words cut her off, "Then why not trust me?"

To her astonishment she blurted, "Because, I'm not sure if you're a problem solver or a schmoozer."

He laughed all the way back to his seat.

A waiter discreetly topped their glasses with champagne.

As if it were a cue, she took a few sips of the tasty drink.

Jared asked, "What are your other opinions of meeting the man behind your assignment?"

Cassandra giggled. Perhaps, she had too much of the bubbly, because she gave him a coquettish look and flippantly replied, "I don't think you really want me to answer your query."

"You're right. I'd rather you give your honest opinion of tarot."

She overcame a tipsy sensation by switching her focus to providing sober information. "Their symbols exude Hebrew teachings, Christian virtues, psychological health, and pathways to all three. They might contain the twenty-two paths to the Tree of Life."

"Then why are you afraid to applaud them, shout about their glory, and rejoice in their array of beneficial attributes?"

She studied Jared's interesting face. Although a man he reminded her of the tarot card labeled III, The Empress. He projected a youthful exuberance. He seemed perpetually pregnant with ideas. And it seemed he was always on the threshold of creativity.

A thought crossed her mind and caused her to shiver. *Like Mother Nature, did his projects have the potential to be both productive and destructive?*

His words interrupted her thought. "Where's your faith?"

"I'm Catholic. My religion forbids its members to believe in divining."

"I'll ask you again. What do you believe about tarot?"

"I've already explained tarot is rooted in Judeo-Christian beliefs."

"Don't you think truth can sell?"

"I'm not sure. After all, folks crucified Christ."

He shot back, "But since His resurrection, Christianity has been a growing hit for over two thousand years."

She assumed no matter what she said or what arguments she presented he would counter with reasons to object to her position.

Jared took her hands in his.

His touch was warm, intense, and unnerving. She felt a surge of sexual energy and an uncomfortable vulnerability. She pulled her hands out of his and placed them in her lap.

She tried to shake off her attraction toward Jared by returning her attention to tarot.

She shared, "Visually the cards are masterpieces. Their esoteric symbols offer a plethora of fascinating interpretations, but..."

A rush of ideas, akin to a swarm of bees, buzzed in her head. She experienced an unfamiliar exhilaration. It suddenly felt imperative to defend tarot publically.

She lifted her champagne flute. "To everyone truly understanding tarot."

"Does this mean we have a deal?"

While under the enchanting influence of champagne she announced, "Indeed. I'd like to share in the anticipation and birth of your project. I'm up for the challenge of exposing the occult's role in defaming tarot.

"For a longtime, I've felt the ghost of tarot haunting me. Until now, I didn't understand its message. Presently, I realize I just might be able to help free the ghost by restoring tarot to its dignified place in history."

He tapped her glass and toasted, "To our joint venture. My dear Cassandra, may history bind our professional, union."

Although irrational, a part of her wanted their union to evolve into something much more personal.

Chapter Four

IV
The Emperor

Next morning, dressed in tight fitting pants and a soft nylon blouse, Cassandra sat in the canvas seat of a director's chair and crossed her legs. Self-conscious of revealing her lower curves, she felt glad to be sitting down. She guessed being in the back of the room would mean fewer people would notice her.

Her stomach was in knots. As a wedge-heeled shoe dangled from her right foot, she hoped she appeared nonchalant.

Awake for hours, after a few bites of dry toast, she felt too jittery to finish eating breakfast.

In order to calm her nerves, she turned to her research and focused on the fifth Major Arcana labeled IV, The Emperor.

Tomas had come up to her room, applied her makeup, and styled her hair. They shared a pot of English breakfast tea.

She noticed he seemed troubled. "Is anything wrong?" she asked.

His hands flew up to the sides of his face as he shook his head from side to side. "Goodness me. Are my emotions that transparent?"

She offered, "Maybe if you talked about them you'd feel better."

He stopped what he was doing and peered into her eyes. "I share an apartment with my best friend and my worst enemy. Just before leaving this morning, we had yet another fight. Without either of us apologizing, she stormed out of the house and went for a run without me."

"What did you argue about?"

"Maybe it's because I have to be so precise at work, but when I'm home I like to relax, unwind. I just can't stand her putting my stuff away. I've told her over and over again to stop imposing her compulsions on me. Don't get me wrong. I'm far from a slob, but I'm not Mr. Neat-Nick either. So what if I leave an unwashed dish in the sink or the New York Times sprawled out on the kitchen table? What harm am I doing? Sure, she's the one who scrubs the shower, vacuums the floors, and washes our clothes, but I do my bit, too. I'm the guy who picks up groceries, fixes the plumbing. Gee, I even change burnt out light bulbs."

He grunted. "In her opinion, by me doing silly, unconscious, little things I'm deliberately disrespecting her."

"So you're a runner?"

"Sort of. I'm more of a jogger. Besides keeping me somewhat healthy, it's something we enjoy doing together."

"Ever have a pebble in one of your running shoes?"

"On occasion."

"What did you do?"

"Of course, I've stopped and removed the stone."

His face took on a confused expression.

She ignored his nonverbal question and asked one of her own. "Why didn't you just leave the little object in your shoe?"

"Because it hurt."

"What would've happened if you left the pebble there indefinitely? What would the stone do to your foot?"

"Irritate it."

"Well my guess is you leaving the unwashed dish in the sink or the newspaper on the kitchen table is like a little pebble in your friend's shoe. It's simply irritating."

Tomas lowered his head and kissed Cassandra on the tip of her nose. "You're brilliant. Thank you for helping me see the light."

Somewhat embarrassed by his reaction, she changed the subject by asking, "What should I wear to the studio?"

"Unless you're being filmed you can wear just about anything. Folks are pretty informal on the set. Comfortable clothes make most sense. Would you like me to call Margo to advise you?"

Cassandra declined his offer. She chose an outfit and hoped the loose blouse would compensate for the clinging pants.

Looking at the crew, she felt overdressed. Most of the guys were wearing jeans and tee shirts. The women, also in jeans, wore pretty tops.

Three cameras partially obstructed the set. From what she could see, the scene looked inviting. Wood paneled walls, dark planked flooring and black leather wingchairs reminded her of a man's study.

The studio was a bustling place. An artistic energy buzzed through the air.

Several individuals were scurrying about moving furniture, adding accessories, flipping through papers attached to clip boards, and adjusting microphones.

Voices mingled in an indistinct, chaotic chant.

From behind her, she heard Jared greet the crew. "Good morning, everyone. Ready to tape a commercial for an upcoming segment?"

Cassandra peered over her shoulder and smiled at him.

He approached and patted her head. "I'm anxious to hear your honest appraisal of my intro."

Before Cassandra could say a word, several people surrounded him.

One by one, they asked Jared questions or presented him with problems.

"Do you want the lighting to remain the same through the concluding remarks or would you like shadows to fade in and out at specific times?"

"Would you prefer footage recapping the guests' credentials?"

"Remember Tina Albright, author of *Proven Near-Death Experiences*? Her publicist insists on having a photo shoot of you two or he'll withdraw permission for her name or works to be mentioned during any upcoming broadcasts."

Jared addressed each issue in turn. He calmly gave clear answers and specific instructions. He listened to suggestions and respectfully evaluated the pros and cons of differing opinions. He modified a few items, and delegated tasks.

As Jared spoke, Cassandra observed his creative and rational sides merging. Like The Emperor tarot card, Jared seemed to symbolize temporal power. *Fact or Truth* was his creation. His staff deferred to him for guidance. They trusted his wisdom to ensure the program's success.

Jared asked one woman. "How's your husband doing?"

"He's slowly improving."

"If there's anything I can do to help please let me know."

"Thank you. You've already done so much by paying for an in-home nurse."

"That was selfish of me. I wanted you to feel comfortable while you were on the set."

Cassandra liked his fatherly style and display of humility.

Jared turned to her. "Best go to makeup to get pretty for the taping."

She watched him stop at the set turning one of the wingchairs toward the camera and pushing the other two to the side.

A woman's voice caused Cassandra to redirect her attention.

"Hi. I'm Bev, the script director."

"Cassandra." She stood and shook the attractive woman's hand. "Nice to meet you."

"I understand you'll be cohosting the segment on tarot."

Cassandra felt uneasy. "I can't image myself on television. Maybe Jared will revise his plan and won't use me in that particular capacity."

Bev chuckled. "Don't worry. He's not some prima donna type. None of us tiptoes around him. Personally, I find it best to be direct and speak my mind. Jared knows the television business, is consistent, and definitely the stable backbone of the show. Fortunately, he's not just creative. He's rational."

"Thanks for your input."

"Anytime. You should also know Jared's extremely guarded. He probably won't tell you much about his past, but it clearly influences his behaviors. If need be, he can fight like a street hoodlum in order to win."

Tempted to ask for details about his aggressive side, Cassandra didn't want to partake in gossiping. She tried to change the subject. "There're a lot more people on the set than I imagined. What does everyone do?"

"Honey, the list is too long for me to know all the staff's duties by heart. Haven't you ever seen credits after a movie?"

"Sure. It goes on and on."

"Well it takes almost as many people to make a television show."

"I'm surprised."

"Guess you think we all make a bundle and have cushy jobs?"

"I'm sure each person adds special talents and deserves to be well compensated."

"You're right, but sadly the lot of us are overworked and underpaid. A decent day is fourteen hours. Most are sixteen. I've even pulled a few twenty-seven hour ones."

"But why?"

"We have to meet our deadlines. If not, the execs drop our series faster than the proverbial hot potato. When that happens, some of us are out of work."

Cassandra wondered why Jared hadn't given her a timeline. Why had he requested she spend the day at the set? Did he expect her to do research before and after she wasted time getting a makeover, going to a bar, and now sitting while everyone else was busy? Did he expect her to work fourteen plus hour days?

"Doesn't anyone complain?"

"Sure, but not out loud. There's an unending stack of applicants representing skilled people waiting to fill our positions."

"How do you deal with the pressure?"

"Work hard. Play hard. That's my philosophy."

"Who are the folks sitting to the left of the stage? I haven't noticed any of them moving. Do they help do things around here?"

"Jared also employs extras. Most don't get to help with the production, but it keeps them off the streets for the day and gives them some cash to find a place to sleep for a few nights."

As Bev walked away, she winked and said, "Have fun."

Seconds later the lights flickered. The space became quiet.

Cassandra sat down and waited. Once again, one of her shoes dangled. Worrying it might drop with a clunk Cassandra carefully put both feet on a rung under her seat.

An overhead monitor lit up with a picture of Jared sitting on one of the wingchairs. The camera zoomed in on his face. With visible lines and wrinkles, he appeared older on screen than in person.

He began reciting scripted dialogue. His furrowed brow added to his wise appearance. She listened to him weave conjecture with fact to the point of it being impossible to separate the two.

His voice clearly spouted bullet points.

"I warn you. It's wise to reserve judgments in accepting our accounts."

"Consider the notion of wisdom and knowledge being two sides of the same coin."

"What about faith and hope? Aren't they united?"

"The big question remains." He paused for theatrical effect. "Which is more important religion or science?"

His lips formed a reassuring grin.

"Perhaps, there's no need to separate the two. Perhaps, science will one day explain religious beliefs.

"Find out on the upcoming episodes of *Fact or Truth.*

She was astounded. Yet she pondered, *Was he a mere opportunist seeking to shape his television destiny? Or did he sincerely hope to enhance the world by joining spiritual and scientific aspects together?*

Chapter Five

V
The Pope

On Thursday evening, Cassandra phoned her mother.

"I have a special assignment and need to devote a great deal of time to my research."

Her mother was quiet for a moment. When she spoke, her voice conveyed sadness. "You're cancelling this weekend's visit. Aren't you? Is that why you sent me the pretty bouquet?"

"Of course not, Mom."

"I guess I'll have to prepare for the Women Club's breakfast by myself."

Cassandra had forgotten all about her promise to help her mother. Feeling ashamed Cassandra added, "Even though I should stay here and work I wouldn't miss your club's event."

All day Friday and into Saturday's early hours Cassandra researched the tarot card labeled V, The Pope.

She informed Margo she was going away for the weekend and wouldn't be needing her, Tomas, or the limo driver's services.

Cassandra planned to rise early Saturday morning, remove the bright nail enamel from her finger and toenails, take the subway back to her apartment, and change into old clothes.

After oversleeping, she scratched that idea.

Cassandra jumped in the shower. Not having time to blow-dry and style her hair, she left it natural. Long ringlets cascaded down her back. She pulled most of it into a ponytail, but a few curly strands managed to escape the elastic tie and seductively framed her pretty face.

She put on the most casual of her outfits, applied cream to her face, and added lip-gloss.

She stepped into flat shoes.

She packed a bag with a simple dress, a sweater, a nightgown, under garments, and her deck of tarot cards.

A cheerful doorman greeted her at the front entrance of the hotel, "Just enough time to get in and out of a cab before the thunderstorm arrives."

Cassandra looked at the charcoal sky. As if in an angry brawl, the clouds seemed to be knocking into each other.

A cabbie took her suitcase. "Where to Miss?"

Holding on to her computer bag and purse, she said, "Grand Central Station."

The taxi crawled along the crowded streets.

"Is there a problem?" she asked.

"Hate to be the bearer of bad news, but an accident in the vicinity has traffic backed up. It'll be a while before we clear the jammed area."

"No problem."

"Nice of you to understand."

"Why wouldn't I?"

"I'm used to people getting upset with me. If I can't get them to where they want to go in a hurry they blame me. I realize important, busy people travel in the city. And I know it's my job to get them places fast."

"I'm surprised any folks would be demanding."

"Are you kidding, lady? I get yelled at, cursed at, and stiffed without a tip more times than I can count. No matter what the traffic's like it's always my fault.

"Other cabbies tell jokes or stories to make the time pass, but whatever I say doesn't work at making people happy. I wish I knew how to win people over. I wish I knew how to make people laugh or at least smile. Some nights I come home thinking I'm all wrong for the job."

"I notice you have a picture on your dash." She looked at two cute, young children feeding a few chickens."

"They're my little angels. I took the snap when they visited my parents' farm."

She could see him smiling in the rearview mirror. "What do you think would happen if I put that adorable photo in a pig sty?"

He laughed, "The pigs would trample it with mud."

"So even though the picture of your children is special to you, pigs wouldn't care. They'd just continue being pigs treating the photograph disrespectfully."

"Sure. They wouldn't know any better."

"Your rude customers remind me of pigs."

Even with the heavy traffic, she arrived at the station with plenty of time to spare.

When she tried to tip the cabbie he said, "Lady you already gave me the biggest tip I've gotten in a longtime."

When he carried her suitcase to the curb, without him noticing, she slipped the tip money behind the picture on his dashboard.

At the departing platform, she boarded the train and walked through the cars until she found a window seat facing the advancing direction.

Once seated, she opened her computer and continued her research.

While the train rolled over miles of track, she lost internet service. Cassandra closed both her laptop and her eyes.

She tried to think of a way to explain the merits of researching tarot to her mother. Without success, she opened her eyes and peered out the window.

As if stalking her, the dark sky followed her all the way to New Haven, Connecticut.

Fearing it was a bad omen she shivered.

Instead, of having Cassandra transfer to a local train, her mother insisted on meeting her at the larger station.

As Cassandra stepped down from the car, she spied her mother standing on the platform.

They walked toward each other and hugged.

Her mother quickly slipped out of their embrace and moved back. "Let me look at you. I've never seen that outfit before." She shook her head. "Oh my, your curly hair reminds me of a bad hair day at the beach." She reached for her daughter's hands. "And your nails, they're like witches' claws."

Cassandra felt her self-confidence shrinking.

Her mother raised her voice, "What on earth possessed you to leave the house looking like that?"

Not wanting to provide too much information, Cassandra answered, "It was my new stylist's idea."

A clap of thunder seemed to admonish Cassandra for telling a half-truth.

"Where're your glasses? No wonder you don't know how... you look."

"I'm wearing contact lenses."

"You've certainly made drastic changes since you visited a few weeks ago. Why? What's wrong?"

Cassandra didn't respond.

"You don't mind if we go straight to the church hall? There's just so much to do before tomorrow morning."

Relieved the inspection was over, Cassandra said, "I'm all yours."

They drove from New Haven to the affluent, seaside town of Old Saybrook.

Cassandra and two other women helped her mother set up folding tables and chairs. They washed the tabletops and covered them with pastel, cloth tablecloths. They wrapped silverware in colorful napkins and made centerpieces with fresh and dried flowers.

Hours later, her mother said, "Kathryn is driving Tess home. And I'd like to visit a friend who I just learned is feeling poorly. If she needs groceries, I might be awhile. Can you keep working? I'll help you finish up when I return."

"Sure, Mom." Cassandra smiled thinking about her mother's charitable nature. No matter how busy she always found or rather made time to be of service to others. In this way, her mother truly lived her faith.

While Cassandra was putting the final touches on the last centerpiece, Father Jorge came into the hall. "Looks lovely."

"Thank you." She asked, "Do you have a few minutes?"

"Of course, my child."

He pulled out a chair and sat across from her.

Cassandra immediately felt guilty bothering him especially on the weekend when he heard confessions and said Mass. The poor man was aging and probably should be resting.

His lips curled upward forming a warm smile.

She marveled at how he always seemed cheerful and available to members of his flock.

She wondered, *Did he feel annoyed by people's silly unending questions? Would he think she was ridiculous wanting his help for such a trivial matter? Or was he, like her mother, genuinely patient?*

He tilted his head in her direction indicating he was ready to listen.

Cassandra rushed her words together. "I'm an historian and am working on an assignment researching tarot cards. My problem is I'm not sure how to tell my mother."

"I don't understand."

"I might cohost a television show and present research debunking the occult's use of tarot."

"Do you feel any part of your work is sinful?"

"No, but I don't want to upset my mom. I was hoping there was something you could say to make the situation easier."

"You must do as you conscience dictates. I can only tell you the Catholic Church's position on tarot. A position, I suspect, you're already well aware of."

He wasn't judgmental or condescending. Like the Major Arcana tarot card called the Pope, he took on the role of an advisor, a friend, and a spiritual protector. Emulating the Holy Father's caring spirit, Father Jorge repeated papal opinion.

As she listened, she longed for his sense of peace. It was as if, for him, revelation and reason were one in the same.

"I appreciate your time, Father."

He rose, and pushed the chair under the table.

He pointed toward the door. "I see your mother's back. Good luck my child. I'll pray for you."

She shook his hand. "I appreciate your offer to speak to God on my behalf."

He gave her fingers a slight squeeze. "Trust, through the grace of God, you shall find answers."

On the ride from the church hall to her parents' house, like a harbinger of doom, rain pounded the roof of the car.

Her mother came straight to the point. "Tell me all about your new assignment."

"I'm doing research for a television producer. The network booked me a suite, as their guest, at the Plaza Hotel. It's such a grand building. Maybe you and Dad could come to visit. I'd love to take you to afternoon tea at their signature restaurant, The Palm Court. Its stained glass ceiling is phenomenal."

The pouring rain limited their visibility.

Her mother turned the windshield wipers to high. "Why do you have to stay at a hotel?"

Cassandra found her speech accelerating. "Since I may narrate parts of the segment the producer, Jared Ashbel, wants me to work closely with his staff writers."

"Oh, I see. What's the show called? What's the subject of your research?"

Cassandra tried to swallow the lump in her throat. She waited until her mother turned the car into the driveway.

When she removed the car keys from the ignition, the repetitive whishing sound stopped.

Her mother wearing a gleaming smile faced Cassandra. "I'm dying to hear all about your work."

"The show is called *Fact or Truth*. Have you seen any episodes?"

"No I haven't, but we'll be sure to tune into yours. What's it about?"

"The segment will focus on the original meaning of tarot cards."

Her mother's smile drooped into a scowl. She began to tremble. She reached for Cassandra's hands. "Unless you stop your research at once, I fear something evil will befall you."

Cassandra's father holding an umbrella opened the passenger door. "Hi there. Glad you were able to come this weekend. Your mom really needs you."

Cassandra stepped out of the car, stood on her tiptoes, and kissed his cheeks.

"I'll be okay. Use the umbrella for mom."

He quickly ran around the car and opened the driver's door.

Rain pelted down.

As Cassandra retrieved her bag, she heard her mother shout, "Your daughter is dabbling in witchcraft."

Without changing his facial expression, her father suggested, "Let's go inside where it's dry."

Once inside the house, they sat in Cassandra's favorite room, the screened in sun porch. Decorated with lounge chairs, small tables, and colorful birdhouses—most of which her father had built—it offered an outdoorsy ambiance.

Twenty-seven years earlier, her parents used a VA loan to purchase the fourteen hundred square foot bungalow where Cassandra grew up. As property values increased so too did property taxes. Although they no longer had mortgage payments, her parents still had to budget their money carefully. Only due to them both working and her father's skills, did they manage to maintain and update their charming dwelling.

Cassandra explained, "I'm simply researching tarot cards. I'm not worshiping them."

Her mother snapped back, "Not yet."

"Mom, did you know their original intent was spiritual?"

Her mother didn't reply.

Cassandra continued, "Unfortunately, many people have misconceptions about the decks. They believe the cards themselves are evil, but that's not so. In addition to Judeo-Christian significance and used in parlor games, the cards may have offered players psychological insights. For hundreds of years the decks had nothing to do with fortunetelling. More recently, the occult corrupted them."

"The Catholic Church clearly forbids them. If we disobey the church we'll no longer have our Lord's protection."

"I think you're selling God short. He's always there for us even if we stray and even if we sin."

"Cassie, if you open the door for the devil to enter no one will be able to save your soul."

"I don't believe in a devil."

"Then who instigates murder, war, greed, or meanness?"

"People do a pretty good job of conjuring up evil on their own. They don't need an outside force to prod them into doing dastardly deeds."

Her mother crossed herself. "Lord, help you. I knew you moving to the big city would prove dangerous."

"Mom, did you know in 1571 Pope Pius V asked the faithful to say the Rosary asking Blessed Mother to intercede and pray for his army to win battles against a larger Muslim fleet. He called the Christians' victory Our Lady of Victory for God."

"What's wrong with that?"

"Whether necessary or not, have you ever heard of a good war?"

"Of course not."

"Yet you don't think the Rosary is bad, because people prayed the sacred beads in order for the pope's troops to be victorious."

Her mother stood and placed her hands on her hips. "I think you'd better remove those contacts and put on your glasses. Maybe then you'll see this tarot thing has distorted your world view."

Her father's calm voice ended the subject. "I trust our daughter will find the right path. She's been well educated in Catholicism. We can resume this discussion later, but for now let's eat. I'm starving."

The topic of tarot didn't come up at the dinner table.

After the dishes were dried and the kitchen was tidy, Cassandra tried to give her mother a hug.

Her mother gently pushed her back.

Cassandra said, "I spoke to Father Jorge about me researching tarot."

"And... "

"And he left the decision of continuing or not up to me."

Without speaking her mother left the room.

Next morning at Mass, the choir sang John D. Becker's *Lead Me Lord*. The words 'Lead me, Lord, lead me, Lord. by the light of truth to seek and find the narrow way' reminded Cassandra the right path wasn't usually the easiest. Problem was, in her predicament, any road she chose was rocky.

Cassandra wasn't sure if she could make a decision without considering what other people felt or thought. She didn't want to offend or frighten her mother. She didn't want to disappoint Mrs. Jansen. She didn't want to sound like a hick town girl to sophisticated Jared Ashbel.

Trying to please everyone seemed impossible.

In her confused state, it was difficult to separate what her conscience was thinking from what her heart was feeling.

Since she moved away from home, Cassandra only attended Mass when visiting her folks. She frequently justified her lax participation to her mother by saying, "Going to Mass is an invitation not an obligation."

While she sat in the crowded pew, she wondered if her familiarity with the ritual led to inattentiveness and was the reason she didn't choose to come more frequently.

Sitting in her hometown church, she tried to have an open mind while concentrating on the meaning of the ceremony.

She watched Father Jorge as he spoke to God and consecrated the Holy Eucharist. She listened to him speak God's word to the assemblage as he read the Gospel. She admired his position of being able to go back and forth between the Supreme Being and the parish members.

She, once again, thought about the Major Arcana called The Pope and wondered, *Did the priest see the face of God in each of us?*

If so, like the card implied, did he think each of us was extraordinary?

Following the service, she helped replenish trays at the Ladies' Club buffet breakfast. Friendly faces greeted her. Most women complimented her updated appearance. Some inquired about her life in New York City.

Thinking she'd be chided, Cassandra didn't tell anyone about her current project.

While sitting next to her mother, she felt tempted to take a poll regarding tarot. She realized, even if every woman in the room embraced the cards, her overprotective mother would tenaciously hold onto her paranoid position in an attempt to keep Cassandra safe.

She knew her mother well. Apprehension defined her daily demeanor.

Cassandra thought about her first day of kindergarten. Rather than her mother reassuring Cassandra, Cassandra had to reassure her mom. Similar scenarios occurred every time Cassandra started a new venture.

Her mother often said, "I can't help it. I was born to worry."

At the train station, her mother warned, "Be careful. Don't lose sight of what's good."

Cassandra wanted to remind her mother of the repetitive Bible lesson, 'fear not', but didn't want to sound disrespectful. "I love you, Mom. Thanks for an interesting weekend."

Once aboard the train, Cassandra chose to sit in a half-full car. She hoped the mesmerizing hum of the wheels skipping along the tracks would help clarify her muddled thoughts. She looked out the window watching the sun slip lower in the sky.

Like the sun, she felt her hopes setting.

She thought, *Maybe this is a sign, but of what?*

Cassandra began to chuckle.

Was she as superstitious as her mother was?

How ironic. Catholic raised women swayed by make-believe rubbish, unimportant concerns, a whole lot of foolishness, and nonexistent threats. A chilling thought went through her mind, *Maybe neither she nor her mother had enough faith.*

In years past, Cassandra focused on attempting to reduce her mother's anxiety. In the process, Cassandra denied her own angst.

In caring what other people thought and trying to satisfy her desire to please everyone, Cassandra ignored her personal preferences.

Along with her changed appearance, Cassandra needed to change her perspective. It was about time she trusted herself. Why shouldn't she when she knew the difference between right and wrong?

After the train arrived in New York City, as Cassandra walked through Grand Central Station, she had the uncanny feeling someone was watching her. She looked over her shoulder but didn't recognize any faces.

Rather than leaving the terminal, she sat on a wooden bench and watched people rushing by.

No one stood out or appeared to be interested in her.

She was just being paranoid.

She wondered if she was more like her mother than she was willing to admit.

Chapter Six

VI
The Lovers

As soon as Cassandra entered her hotel room, she caught sight of a blinking red light on the phone. She assumed the call was from her mother.

Not feeling ready to hear her mother's distraught, worried voice, Cassandra decided to unpack, and take a bath before picking up the message. She felt she needed time to prepare her words carefully. Rather than sounding offensive, she wanted to express appreciation for her mother's concerns. She wanted to reassure her mother everything would turn out for the best.

Following a long soak in the marble tub, wearing a provocative nightgown—one she would never have purchased—and with her hair slightly damp Cassandra felt refreshed enough to hear a litany of her mother's warnings.

Before the hour was too late, she decided to listen to the call.

To her surprise, the message was from Jared.

"Your driver will pick you up at nine-thirty tomorrow morning. We'll be flying to Italy where you can continue your research. Pack light. And don't forget to bring your passport."

Her mother's urgings to withdraw from the tarot assignment flew from Cassandra's mind.

She listened to the message two more times before believing her lifelong dream of going to Italy was about to come true.

Fortunately, two years earlier when her parents suggested they drive to Niagara Falls for a family trip,

Cassandra applied for and received a passport. Unfortunately, when she reminded her mother of the post 911 rules about needing a passport to enter Canada, her mother said, "We won't be crossing the border. I wouldn't dare leave US soil."

Cassandra never had a chance to use her passport. Her modest salary barely covered her living expenses. A big part of her income went to pay rent. Student loan payments gobbled up the remainder. She seldom could afford any extras and she certainly wasn't in a position to travel.

After placing the receiver back in its cradle, she twirled around the sitting room until she danced her way into the bedroom.

Her studies acquainted her with data dating from antiquity to the modern age. Several research assignments afforded her opportunities to conduct in-depth reviews of specific Roman and Italian periods. She viewed untold numbers of photographs, illustrations, and maps of different parts of Italy.

Important Italian personalities paraded through her mind. She thought of Italian explorers, painters, sculptors, artists, opera stars, popes, film directors, and actors.

With her head overloaded with names, faces, and places, she collapsed onto her bed. Tears of joy slipped down from her wide opened eyes to the tips of her smiling lips.

She recalled romantic stories of lovers walking through ancient ruins, bicycling along azure coastlines, and sunbathing on exotic Italian isles.

A tug from her rational side stopped her daydreaming. She needed to pack.

She jumped off the bed. From a shelf in her closet, she pulled down a large red and white herringbone patterned suitcase and unzipped it. Inside was another case. In one of its pockets was a matching folded cloth bag.

Cassandra decided to use the two smaller pieces.

She tried on one outfit after another, but couldn't decide what to take with her. The room quickly resembled a teenager's with sweaters, blouses, skirts, dresses, and pants littered about.

She considered taking the larger suitcase, but decided she shouldn't. She told herself this was a business trip and probably a brief one. There probably wouldn't be time to sightsee, stroll through museums, go to theaters, or sample food from many restaurants.

One by one, she placed majority of her clothes back in the closet and in drawers. She folded her favorites and squeezed them into the case. Regardless of their lack of practicality, while being in *bella Italia* she wanted to feel attractive.

Minutes after midnight, she packed the cloth bag with nightgowns, a few cosmetics, jewelry, and her Visconti-Sforza tarot deck.

She went to bed, but was too excited to sleep. At six-thirty, a room service waiter delivered cereal, fruit, and a pot of tea to her room.

After eating, she phoned her mother's number. The call went to voicemail. Cassandra left a message, "I'm flying to Italy to do research. I'll call you after I arrive. Love you and Dad."

She had just stepped out of the shower when Tomas arrived to fix her hair and apply her make-up.

He was almost as giddy as she was. "Love traveling, don't you?"

"Are you coming with us?"

"Sadly, I'm not. I've packed sample sized hair products and makeup. I've listed the sequence of cosmetics I apply to your face. I've also given you suggestions of what to use during the day and in the evenings." He handed her a black patent leather box. He opened it and showed her the contents. "Everything you'll need is in here." He attached a shoulder strap.

Before leaving, he kissed her on both cheeks. "Have fun, sweetie. And thanks again for your advice. I'm trying real hard not to put pebbles in my roommate's shoes."

"Good for you and your friend."

After he left, Cassandra checked her purse one more time. She had her credit card, and a debt card. Online she read about using these cards to get Euros from Italian ATM machines. She pulled out her passport and turned the blank pages hoping to, someday, see them filled with stamps from around the world. With great pleasure, she put her passport securely in her purse's zipped pocket.

She removed cosmetics from the cloth bag and filled the space with her computer. At nine-twenty, Cassandra, with the lightweight bag's strap over one shoulder and the cosmetics' luggage strap over the other, wheeled the bright suitcase to the elevator.

Before her conversation with the driver advanced beyond pleasantries, he pulled into an underground parking structure of a building a few streets from the hotel.

He parked next to an elevator, exited the vehicle, and opened the passenger door. "I'll get your luggage."

"Where're we going?"

"To the rooftop heliport."

When the elevator opened, Jared was waiting for her.

He was dressed in jeans and a sweatshirt.

She wondered about her choice of wearing a fur-trimmed cardigan, tapered trousers, and spiked heels.

He greeted her, "Good morning. You look lovely."

She felt her cheeks burn and hoped he didn't notice her blushing.

He took her hand.

She felt on edge and anxiously wondered how she'd be able to carry on a conversation with him.

He ushered her into a four-place helicopter. "Hope you don't mind the tight accommodations. It's a lot quicker than driving to the airport."

As the helicopter flew over the city, Cassandra was too enthralled to be nervous. Like a young child, she peered out the bubble glass and pointed left then right. "Feels like I'm sitting on a magic chair rising higher and higher in the air. It's as if I can almost reach out and touch the tops of the skyscrapers."

"Is this your first time in a helicopter?"

"It's my first time flying."

"Do you like it?"

She giggled. "It's exhilarating to get a bird's eye view of the city."

While she raved about the sights, she felt his eyes watching her. She tried to act reserved by withholding her comments. Before long, she couldn't contain her excitement. She clapped her hands. "This is fabulous."

She quickly clasped them and put them in her lap. "Sorry."

His smile was warm and appeared genuine. "Don't feel inhibited. It's refreshing to see your enthusiasm."

At JFK airport, they boarded a private jet.

As she stepped into the cream-colored interior, she involuntarily gasped. "Is this your plane?"

"No. It belongs to the network." He placed his hand on a headrest above a spacious seat. "Although the view will remain static for most of the trip, for takeoff and landing I think you'll prefer a window seat on this side of the plane."

She followed his suggestion.

He slid into the seat next to hers.

Almost immediately, a flight attendant wheeled a cart down the aisle. Topped with a canister, silver ice bucket, and a crystal bowl filled with black caviar surrounded by thin crackers, she stopped the cart next to Jared.

She released individual trays from their right armrests. She took the lid off the canister and using small tongs removed two steamy towels for Cassandra and Jared to wash their hands.

From a lower shelf, the attendant produced white linen placemats, napkins, cutlery, plates and champagne flutes.

As she was about to pour champagne into their stemware, Cassandra held up her hand. "I'd rather have water with no ice."

The attendant glanced at Jared. "None for me either."

He turned to Cassandra, "Are you feeling okay?"

She nodded. "I don't want anything to dull my senses."

She leaned her head on the windowpane. She peered at a man removing her luggage from a small truck.

The flight attendant redirected her attention by serving Cassandra a glass of water.

She drank it in a few gulps.

Jared topped a few crackers with caviar, put them on his plate, and passed it to Cassandra.

"No, thank you. I don't like the fishy taste." She scrunched up her nose. "Sorry, I haven't cultivated a palate for the finer things in life."

"Don't apology. I appreciate your honesty." He put the plate on the cart.

Jared's arms reached under her tray. "I'll just fasten your seatbelt. We'll be taking off shortly."

His slight touch sent a warm sensation to drift through her body.

She caught a whiff of the clean scent of his shampoo and felt a delightful tingling dance from her toes to her fingertips.

Her hand reached for her seatbelt buckle as she said, "I'd like to learn…"

As his hand guided hers in completing the simple task, her eyes met his intense pair. She felt as if they had cast a spell causing her to fall into their seductive depths. Automatically she licked her lips.

The flight attendant interrupted them. "Came to collect your dishes." She cleared their trays and slipped them back in the armrests.

The plane began to taxi.

Cassandra stared out the window. "I'm glad we're traveling during the day."

When the plane took off, intent upon watching the structures beneath them growing smaller and smaller, she didn't seem to notice the steep ascent.

Soon the plane entered a cloudbank.

Sunlight filtered through the mist.

Cassandra briefly turned toward Jared. "This is my vision of Heaven, bright, soft, and fluffy."

The plane rose above the clouds and leveled off. It flew through clear blue skies.

He reached over their heads and pressed the flight attendant's call button. "At the moment, my idea of heaven is having lunch."

Like a genie, the attendant seemed to appear from nowhere. She wheeled a cart topped with two oversized salads.

Jared and Cassandra munched on baby greens, mixed with creamy goat cheese, caramelized mushrooms, and fresh tomatoes, accompanied by warm black olive focaccia bread.

When Jared finished eating he asked, "How's your research going?"

"Starting from zero, I've been analyzing each of the twenty-two Major Arcana or trump cards in great detail.

I've compiled data on the first six and am currently studying the seventh."

"Which means you're working on the Major Arcana labeled VI. What's it called?"

"The Lovers."

He giggled. "Really."

She surmised he was an experienced flirt. Yet, she couldn't help be stimulated by his polished seductive moves. She channeled her desire by focusing on her research. She passed her dish to Jared, closed her tray, reached under her seat for the cloth bag, unzipped a pocket, and pulled out her tarot deck. "I'll show you the Lovers."

She removed a card and put it on his tray. "As you can see the top figure is wearing a blindfold. You've probably guessed he's Cupid."

"So love is blind."

"Maybe, but at this stage, Cupid can't see if love will or will not develop. The card implies the dawn of love or the promise of love. Cupid is standing on a fountain implying any relationship, like water, is fluid."

"Is the couple smitten with passion?"

"Not necessarily. The man and woman, holding hands and gazing into each other's eyes reflect love as the noblest sentiment we humans can experience. It can refer to a deep friendship, high esteem for someone, as well as emotional and/or physical affection."

"Are you saying, this card could represent our budding relationship? What I mean is, while the show is in-between seasons you and I can get to know each other."

Was it obvious she felt infatuated by this rogue?

His words were sobering. "I admire your intellect and hope we can develop an enduring friendship."

She felt disappointment pierce her infatuation and bring her back to reality. She continued to share the card's symbols. "When two people meet, anything can happen between them. Cupid, a winged creature, can fly away in an instant and leave them, or he can shoot the couple with one of his darts. The card is more about the promise of love than what the couple share in the moment. In the future, they may become friends, have an amorous encounter, or commit to each other in matrimony." She paused. "And there are negative possibilities as well."

"Such as?"

She peered into his eyes trying to observe his reaction to her words, "Such as, infidelity, betrayal, unrequited love." His noncommittal stare didn't give her any clues regarding his thoughts.

His gaze shifted to the card.

She offered additional information. "In a biblical sense the card represents Adam and Eve."

"The first lovers."

"Unaware of their paradise they felt discontent with the Garden of Eden. They ate fruit from the tree of the Knowledge of Good and Evil. By doing so they saw what didn't exist in their world."

"Evil."

She nodded. "When they learned of evil they appreciated what existed in the garden."

"Goodness."

"Each of us is like Adam and Eve. We have difficulty appreciating the blessings in our lives."

He turned to her. "Is that true for you, too?"

Unsure of what she presently had she hesitated. She focused on the moment. "I'm grateful for this trip. How about you?"

"By being discontent with what I've achieved, I'm probably taking my good fortune for granted." He snickered. "Should I expect banishment as a punishment?"

"The card implies God is protective not punitive. It appears by God sending Adam and Eve into the world He gave them the opportunity to learn humility. Thus, the card begs the question, in Adam and Eve's story is seeking knowledge merely evil or is it something more?"

"How so?"

"The card encourages us to examine the roles we played in our past, are playing in the present, and how we can act in the future. In short, the message is introspection and choice can lead to maturity and a path back to God."

"So the card deviates from the biblical story. I noticed there isn't a snake in the image. Didn't it tempt Eve and didn't Eve tempt Adam? Wasn't the snake ultimately to blame for their transgressions?"

"The card teaches us blaming is a way to avoid self responsibility."

She stowed the cards away and silently glanced out the window. As Jared had predicted the view remained the same.

He announced, "Time for a snack. Flying always makes me hungry and sleepy." He pressed the flight attendant's call button.

Within seconds, she was at his side. "How can I be of assistance?"

"I'd like three scoops of chocolate ice-cream topped with strawberry syrup, nuts, and lots of whipped cream."

Cassandra laughed. "I'll have a cup of hot herbal tea."

While Jared enjoyed his ice-cream sundae, Cassandra asked, "With such a sweet tooth, how do you stay so slim?"

He shrugged his shoulders. "Don't you have any vices?"

"I love pasta. I can eat it seven days a week and often did while growing up."

He laughed. "Then that's what you'll have for dinner tonight. What's your favorite?"

"Rigatoni with puntesca sauce."

"Really? So you like spicy food."

"Love it."

"Doubt if the attendant can whip up anything fancy."

"As long as she has crushed red pepper and a few other spices, I can turn most marinara sauces into a jazzy arrabbiata sauce. What types of foods did you grow up eating?"

"My mom wasn't much of a cook. Not liking to eat a lot, she prepared bland, non-descript foods. My dad wasn't fussy, but he often brought home Chinese takeout. To this day I can't get enough chow mein."

"So noodles are your favorite, too."

"Never thought of it that way."

Cassandra asked Jared, "Where did the inspiration for your *Fact or Truth* show come from?"

"Guess I just question everything."

As they spent hours discussing various past segments, Cassandra felt her admiration for Jared growing.

Their discussion about near death experiences lasted through dinner.

The attendant served coffee and dessert.

Cassandra took one bite of the cheesecake before pushing it aside.

"Don't you like it?"

"Someday I'll bake you a Visconti cheesecake, but I warn you in advance, it will spoil you."

"Since I ordered this cheesecake from a premiere New York bakery, I can't wait to try your family's recipe."

Jared was napping when the plane began its initial descent. Stars twinkled through the night sky.

The flight attendant came by. She nudged Jared and told him to raise his seat to the upright position.

Cassandra leaned her head against the window watching the twinkling stars. As the plane entered its final descent, an array of lights welcomed them.

"It reminds me of a huge Christmas tree all aglow."

He leaned into her to view the sight.

Enchanted by his closeness she didn't move an inch. She couldn't deny she felt sexually attracted to Jared. She assumed he had a past filled with a string of temporary lovers. Nevertheless, she felt tempted to become his next fling.

Her sense of reason was warning her to resist his advances.

But how could she when she felt she was falling, in Dante words, 'love that moves the sun and the other stars.'

Chapter Seven

VII
The Chariot

In the middle of the night, a black car with tinted windows met Jared and Cassandra at the airport. While it smoothly drove through the streets, she pressed her head against the window, but couldn't see much.

Sometime later, they arrived at a sleek, modern hotel.

She told Jared, "It's not exactly what I expected."

He laughed. "Glad Italy can surprise you."

After checking in at the front desk, they took the elevator to the fourth floor.

The bellman stopped at her room and ushered her inside.

Jared waved. "See you in a few hours or would you rather sleep in."

"When an historic city awaits my discovery I wouldn't dream of wasting time sleeping."

Cassandra unpacked and took a long soak in an oversized tub. Still feeling wired she powered up her computer and researched Milan's history, points of interest, and the city's commercial value to the Italian economy.

Before turning off her nightstand lamp, she intended to examine the Visconti-Sforza's eighth Major Arcana, labeled VII, The Chariot, but as soon as she rested her head on the comfy pillow, she felt overcome with fatigue.

Before she received a wakeup call, she awakened. Strangely, her body felt both rested and restless. Without getting out of bed, she satisfied her urge to study the eighth tarot card. Absorbing its fascinating revelations, she had to pull herself away from it in order to shower, dress, and be on time to meet Jared for breakfast.

In the hotel's restaurant, a sumptuous display of cheeses, cold sliced meats, fresh fruits, and hot rolls covered a long table.

Jared greeted her at the buffet with a cheery, "*Buon Giorno*."

After eating their fill he sipped a frothy cappuccino while she enjoyed a café au lait.

He laid out his plan for the day. "I thought we'd start by visiting the *Duomo* Cathedral followed by a visit to *Santa Maria delle Grazie* where I made reservations to see "The Last Supper" and, if time permits, stop by the *Castello Sforzesco*, Sforza Castle."

Cataloged facts spilt from her lips, "Under the Visconti family rule the Cathedral's construction began in 1386 and extended for another five centuries. It's the most important example of Gothic architecture in Italy."

As if resigning himself to hearing a longwinded commentary, Jared placed his elbows on the table and leaned his chin on his folded hands.

Cassandra elaborated, "The roof has pinnacles and spires set upon delicate flying buttresses. The *Madonnina*—gold colored statue of Mary—is at the highest point. There are three thousand, four hundred statues, one hundred thirty-five gargoyles, and seven hundred figures. With seventy-eight architects overseeing its construction, it's filled with contrasting, sometimes uncomplimentary, styles."

She noticed the glazed look of boredom in his eyes and suggested, "Let's go see it and judge for ourselves."

"We can walk to all three sights from here." As Jared stood, the waiter brought Jared his coat. "Do you want to go to your room to get a jacket?"

"Thinking it was always warm in sunny Italy, I didn't bring one."

"No problem. We're in Italy's fashion district where you'll find clothes from all over the world." He draped his coat over her shoulders.

As they stepped out of the hotel, seconds before they entered the quick flow of heavy foot traffic, he searched for her hand hidden under the woolen fabric. "I don't want to lose you in the crowded city."

Although the air was brisk, she felt a warm glow heat up her body. "Are you cold?" she asked.

"No, not really. Besides, it's only a short distance to our destination."

As people approached, she noticed, regardless of age, most were well dressed.

A block away, standing between other buildings, she caught sight of the massive Cathedral. The magnificent structure rendered her speechless.

In silence, they joined the tourists waiting in queue.

Cassandra peered upward at the marble façade, multitude of spirals, and various statues.

After they entered the sacred space, she removed Jared's coat, handed it to him, and said, "I'd like to say a prayer."

She slipped into a pew and knelt.

She thanked God for their safe flight, her opportunity to visit Italy, and the people who toiled to create this masterful cathedral.

She bowed her head and asked for discernment in making the right judgments regarding her tarot research, her relationship with worldly Jared, and her upcoming future.

While Cassandra could spend days, possibly weeks, studying the details housed in this church Jared took her hand and gently pulled her forward in order to keep pace with the stream of moving visitors.

They climbed the flights of stairs to the top level. They moved along the roof gazing from views across Milan to the snowcapped peaks of the Alps.

Once again, she thought of the thousands of workers who contributed their talents and labor to build this phenomenal edifice. She remembered reading about a canal system especially built to bring tons of pink hued white marble from Lake Maggiore quarries to this site.

She turned to Jared, "I think the meaning of the eighth Major Arcana pertains to this architectural marvel."

He shook his head. "You're conscientious even on vacation."

"I thought the purpose of this trip was to explore tarot."

He shrugged his shoulders. "Right."

"The card labeled the Chariot pictures a crowned queen seated on a two wheeled chariot pulled by winged horses. In Roman military tradition victors paraded around in their chariots while crowds applauded soldiers' triumphs. With a woman at the reins, the card symbolizes a greater celebration of glory and fame. It recognizes success, progress, and great achievement."

She returned her attention to the many details surrounding her and almost forgot about Jared until he piped up. "Let's go do some shopping."

From the Cathedral they crossed the Plazza del Duomo to Milan's glass covered shopping mall, *malliazza della Scala*. Designed in 1861, originally named after Vittorio Emanuele II the first king of the Kingdom of Italy, the Galleria was alive with activity. Its practical aspect—sheltering shoppers from the elements—reflected a blend of precision engineering and artistic symmetry.

They stepped over the central mosaic depicting the bull from the Turin Coat of Arms. While her eyes cast upward at the high glass dome, he took her hand and led her into an exclusive clothing shop.

She didn't feel like shopping, but Jared addressed a saleswoman, "The lady's looking for a jacket."

Having noticed what most women were wearing Cassandra corrected him. "I'd like to see your coat selection."

"This way please."

They followed the woman into a salon. She indicated they sit on one of the crushed velvet, high back chairs.

Another woman served them demitasse and wafers.

Models wearing colorful coats paraded before them.

While each item was stunning, Cassandra's eyes zoomed in on one in particular, a mid-length, red, collarless, swing style.

The observant saleswoman asked the model to remove it. She brought the coat to Cassandra. "Please, try it on."

Her cheeks flushed. Thinking she was inches shorter than the model, she was sure it would make her look like her former frumpy self.

Jared encouraged her. "I like this one, too."

She slipped into the pretty coat.

He walked around her. "It's a perfect fit."

While gazing in a full-length mirror, Cassandra silently agreed. She especially liked the way the bodice accented her upper curves, the graceful lines of the flared skirt, and although the fabric was cashmere it felt like chiffon.

"We'll take it." Jared reached for his wallet and pulled out a credit card.

Cassandra protested, "No, I want to pay for it."

"Please consider it a thank you gift for agreeing to do the tarot segment."

She touched the soft fabric. "Thank you. It's beautiful."

He said, "You not only have excellent taste you tastefully wear your clothes."

Cassandra thought of how she usually dressed. As if to conceal her femininity, she chose oversized, unattractive garments. It was as if she was hiding from the world.

Had she internalized her mother's warnings? To prevent herself from being hurt, did she fear being seen, being touched, being loved?

In covering up her personal assets, Cassandra perpetuated a destructive pattern. She set herself up to be ostracized and isolated.

She realized since she started showing her external self she gained strength to disclose her inner thoughts.

What she didn't recognize was by revealing her true self she obtained the power to prevent herself from becoming victimized.

With a momentary air of confidence, she linked arms with Jared.

They strolled to *Santa Maria delle Grazie.*

He glanced at his watch. "If we hurry, we'll just make our reservation time."

She felt him pulling her along into a slow run.

Along with the throngs of onlookers, they filed in front of Leonardo da Vinci's fifteen by twenty-nine foot mural, *The Last Supper.*

He nudged her shoulder. "I'm aware patron Ludovico Sforza, Duke of Milan commissioned this work."

"I'm impressed. Few people know that fact."

He beamed with an air of pride.

She cleared her throat. "But I'm more impressed with the masterpiece."

He laughed.

She paused opposite Jesus' image for a moment. She felt He was peering into her eyes and communicating with her soul.

Once outside the convent, Jared directed her around the corner to a restaurant. They followed a waiter down a spiral staircase to a small room crowded with tables. She took off her coat, placed it over the back of her chair making sure it didn't drag on the floor.

He ordered *risotto alla Milanese at Rataná*, grated cheesy arborio rice, saffron, white wine, and chicken stock. She had a creamy, buttery Polenta.

"Surprised, you're not having pasta?"

"While I'm here, I want to sample the specialties of the region."

After eating half her lunch, she said, "Hate to admit, this polenta rivals my mom's."

She offered him a taste.

"Um, um good. Try some risotto."

He fed her a spoonful.

Cassandra savored the simple intimacy of sharing food. It made the meal taste extra delicious.

He quipped, "Can't believe you have nothing to say about *The Last Supper*."

"You'll think me silly."

"Try me."

"I felt the painting sent me a message."

His eyes widened.

"It was as if Jesus was telling me, as a Christian, I'm called, like each apostle, to be His disciple."

"In what way?"

"That's still a mystery."

They walked to *Castello Sforzesco*, Sforza Castle. It was an example of defensive architecture with high walls, towers, ramparts, moats, and a covered road. Originally constructed by Galeazzo II Visconti in the thirteen hundreds, Filippo Maria Visconti enlarged it, and Francesco Sforza made it his residency in 1450.

Cassandra paid special attention to their guide's brief narrative, "The notorious Visconti brothers, Giovanni Maria and Filippo Maria were known for their cruelty.

"Giovanni had fits of rage, ordered mass executions often performed by his pack of vicious dogs tearing criminals to bits.

"Following Giovanni's assassination, nineteen year old Filippo became Duke of Milan. He quickly had his brother's assassins executed and married the deceased regent's widow to gain her fortune. When Filippo heard rumors of her infidelity, he had her tortured and killed.

"Extremely superstitious, he had his second wife imprisoned because a dog howled on their wedding night.

"A paranoid, nervous fellow he hid in this fortress. He detested his ugly appearance and avoided people. His love of card games prompted him to commission the first tarot decks.

"He reigned for thirty years. And, he shrewdly betrothed his eight-year old daughter, Bianca Maria to Francisco Sforza, who had fought with and against Filippo's troops for twenty years."

Jared took Cassandra's hand in his and gave it a squeeze. "After hearing about your notorious relatives, I'll bet you could benefit from immersing yourself in Milan's nightlife."

Starting at six, they partook of the *aperitivo* or happy hour. He ordered them Milan's version of *negroni sbagliato*, equal pours of gin, Campari, red vermouth and a splash of Procecco.

He casually asked, "Tell me more about the card you mentioned earlier. The one you're reviewing today?"

She refreshed his memory. "It's the eighth Major Arcana, called the Chariot. The female figure, by carrying a scepter and a golden globe, represents glory."

"And?"

Rather than losing his interest by providing too many details she summarized, "It speaks to the personal victory of meeting life's everyday challenges." She looked beyond him into the room filled with animated men and women. "It's a place I long to reach." She redirected her gaze to his intriguing face. "You, on the other hand, have an extensive list of achievements."

"Making a few dollars doesn't make me a success."

She held up her glass. "A toast to your modesty." She took a sip of the bubbly drink. "The card also alludes to maintaining a high code of ethics."

"Does it have religious implications?"

She nodded. "The Chariot represents God constantly waiting for each of us. He's always ready to whisk us away from our tribulations. All we have to do is seek Him, call His name, and believe in Him to be safely taken away from harm."

Jared didn't comment.

After a few more sips of her cocktail, Cassandra reflected upon her reaction to visiting Sforza Castle. "Now I can understand why no one in my family spoke of our infamous ancestors." She lowered her head. "Like my relatives I, too, am ashamed to be from such a treacherous lineage."

He ordered another round of cocktails. "My notorious relatives were closer to my birth."

She looked up and waited for him to continue.

He downed his drink.

"At seventeen, I found my mother's dead body. She was in the bathtub soaking in water tainted with blood seeping from her slit wrists."

A waitress replaced Jared's empty glass with a fresh *negroni*. She placed another cocktail in the center of the table.

Jared's voice seemed to lack emotion. "I remember my mom playing games with me when I was a kid. She drew upon her astounding imagination to entertain me. But her unpredictable moods made my life a living hell. One minute she was happy. In the next, she was depressed, crying like a baby. She'd lock herself in her room. As I got older, I noticed she'd spend money buying things she didn't need. She went on outrageous shopping sprees. Clothes, still with price tags attached, crammed her closets."

He gulped down the rest of his cocktail and snickered. "My well-intended dad spoke of unconditional love. Maybe he loved my mother unconditionally, but he missed the mark with my sister, Sue and me. He failed to protect us from our mom's irrational anger. She'd rant and rave, call us names, throw things at us, and blame us for her pathetic life. Jealous of Sue's good looks she belittled her, humiliated her, and wounded her soul."

Jared took a sip of the other negroni.

"My pop read the Bible and believed prayer could change all things. But he wasn't so naïve as to ignore professional help. He arranged for my mom to see a psychiatrist. The learned man diagnosed her with bipolar disorder and prescribed medication, but she refused to take it."

His voice became more intense. "What frightened my sister, Sue, most was our mom's eerie laugh and how she'd jeer at us. The vision of her bulging eyes terrified us in the moment, but the sight intruded Sue's dreams turning them into nightmares. She thought our mother was the devil incarnate. Many a night, awakened by the horrific sight of our demented mother's face, my sister crawled into my bed a whimpering mess."

As Jared reached for what was left of the remaining drink. Cassandra took his hand and held it on the tabletop.

He looked in her eyes. "How can I believe in God? He wasn't there to protect my sweet baby sister. He let her believe by mother's evil words. At fifteen, Sue ran away from home. She hated herself to the point of selling her body on the streets."

Cassandra's other hand stroked Jared's cheek.

He briefly glanced up at her. "Sorry. I didn't mean to dump on you. I don't make a habit of revealing my ugly past. In fact, I usually avoid sharing personal information."

His free hand waved through the air.

"Cassandra, you have a strange affect on me. I can't explain it. I see you as a bright light shining through bleak darkness."

"Don't you think God's chariot swept you into a better world?"

"No." He stared into her eyes. "I did that."

She wondered if he really didn't believe in God.

"Rejoicing in my mother's suicide, I left my grieving father. I stupidly believed our mother could no longer hurt me, or my sister. I tried to find Sue, to tell her the happy news. I thought I could save her from herself. When I finally located her, she didn't seem to care. Despite my urgings, rather than coming home, she chose to disappear. She occasionally called. Even as an emotional wreck she cheered me up, encouraged me to finish school, and egged me on to pursue my outlandish career.

"Years after finishing college, when I got a foothold in show biz, I hired private eyes to track her whereabouts. Each time I went to see Sue, she hugged me and promised to change. I gave her money. Later, I found out she used it to buy meth, crack cocaine, or other street junk. During our final meeting, she begged me to give up on her, and forget her. She said she never wanted to see me again.

"And, I haven't seen her since. Last I heard, my damaged sister moved to Brooklyn, was still using drugs, and continued walking into one abusive relationship after another."

Using his free hand, he lifted the glass and drained the last drops of his negroni. "I just couldn't stand hearing about her life, a life I was helpless to change. Selfishly thinking of my feelings, a few years ago I called off the private detectives."

"Sounds like you gave Sue the dignity to make her own choices. Maybe one day she'll choose to seek help."

Without letting go of his hand, Cassandra rose, walked to his side, and embraced Jared.

As she felt his internal, sorrowful sobs, she knew there were no words to comfort him.

Chapter Eight

VIII
Justice

Next morning, in her Milan hotel room, Cassandra awakened with an aching heart. Images of Jared as a young boy confused and frightened by his mother's changing moods flooded her mind.

It wasn't fair for him or any child to fear one parent and feel unprotected by the other.

Before she began getting ready to meet Jared, she walked over to the desk and flipped over the ninth Major Arcana tarot card, labeled VIII, Justice.

She hoped she wasn't rationalizing by believing one day each person would meet with divine justice.

Still, she wished there were limits to anyone exercising free will on earth.

How often were innocent children victims of injustice? She wished God wouldn't allow anyone to harm the helpless little ones. She wished He hadn't allowed His son, Jesus Christ, to be a victim of injustice. Couldn't God the Father come up with a better way to give us eternal salvation?

Her thoughts shifted from the unanswerable to her reality. Feeling gratitude for having loving parents, she reached for her cell.

Her mother answered, "Is everything all right?"

"Things couldn't be better. *Bella Italia* reminds me of great grandmother, Teresa. It's elegant, friendly, and artistic. The food is incredible . You and Dad must visit."

"Maybe someday."

"Just called to say I love you. I want to thank you for my great childhood."

Her mother sniffled. "Stop all this sentimental stuff before you make me cry."

"Okay, but it's true." She paused to let her mother savor the compliment. "Is there anything I can bring you from Milan?"

"Just you along with your restored good sense of reason. I'm looking forward to the day you break ties with the television station." Her voice sounded shaky. "Love you." The line went dead.

She knew her mother's opinion. She believed, as long as Cassandra continued working on the tarot assignment, she put herself in grave danger.

Cassandra's eyes focused on the image of Justice. A woman held a scale in one hand and a two-edged sword in the other. The scales represented the need to keep a balance between desires and values. The sword reflected the precision necessary to slice through difficult situations to make clear judgments.

She pressed the card to her chest and hoped she would be able to fulfill this noble quest.

Glancing at the clock, she placed the card on the bottom of the deck and dashed into the shower.

Half-hour later, the doorman escorted her to a red Ferrai parked along the hotel's circle drive.

Jared sitting behind the wheel greeted her with a broad smile.

She grinned. "I can see you're having a good morning."

He nodded and revved the engine. "Picked the color to match your new coat."

Touching the soft fabric, as she slid into the leather passenger seat, she felt glamorous.

He eased into the slow moving traffic. "We'll head north out of the city. Rather than the expressway, I thought we'd take the back roads to Lake Maggiore. It's fifty-six miles from Milan. There we can visit Visconti's *Castello dal Pazzo*."

"I've seen videos of its restoration. The castle is privately owned and currently used as a wedding venue."

They climbed through winding roads covered with lush vegetation.

He pulled into a parking lot in front of a café.

They each ordered a cup of cappuccino and slices of *panettoni*, a fluffy brioche with candied fruits.

Cassandra gushed. "It's a family tradition to have *panettoni* every Christmas morning. On February third my mother serves us a slice of dry, leftover Christmas *panettoni* for breakfast to ward off the flu and protect our noses and throats."

She wondered what he must think of her superstitious family.

She thought she could avoid hearing his reaction by redirecting his focus. "I love the romantic tale of how the bread originated."

As if waiting for her to continue Jared didn't comment.

Following his silent cue, she felt he had given her permission to elaborate. "Tony, who was an apprentice baker, fell in love with the master baker's daughter. When Tony asked to court the beautiful maiden the master replied, 'Bake me a loaf of bread proving you are worthy of my child.'

"Tony experimented and experimented until he made a loaf expressing the sweet love he felt in his heart. The master examined the dome shaped loaf. He cut a piece and studied the light airy texture. After one bite he gave Tony his blessing to court his daughter and named Tony's creation *panettoni*, Tony's bread."

Jared's cell chimed. He glanced at the screen. "Sorry, I need to take this call." He rose and stepped outside.

When he returned, he told her, "Looks like my *Fact or Truth* show is in danger of being cancelled."

Her initial thought centered on herself. She might not have to present her research results on national TV. Guilt washed over her for being selfish.

She stared at Jared. He didn't show any sign of worry. By now, she realized he was good at hiding his emotions.

Still she resisted an urge to embrace him in an attempt to offer him comfort.

"I thought the show had a history of high ratings."

"But the network is always on the lookout for new series. There's never a shortage of ideas floating across the execs' desks.

"Television's a dog eat dog business. In my hungry days, I didn't hesitate to nip at heels and push people out of my way in order to get to the top."

"Do you know who's vying for your air time?"

"I'm surprised you haven't heard. Bev, my script director has presented a proposal, one I even like."

"Did she come to you first?"

"No, but she didn't do anything I haven't done. It's karma for me to be a victim of someone else's ambition. It's what I deserve."

He ended their discussion by asking, "What's today's tarot card?" He sipped his cappuccino.

"Justice," she said.

He coughed to avoid choking. "How fitting. This tarot stuff is like daily horoscopes. On any given day any of the cards' interpretations are applicable in explaining most circumstances."

She didn't want to get lost in tarot. She wanted to focus on Jared. She wanted him to express his feelings regarding the possibility of losing his show. "What can you do to save the series?"

"Together, we'll have to make the tarot segment a smashing success. If the network doesn't renew the *Fact or Truth* contract, at least my swansong will leave a controversial buzz in its wake.

"Please forgive me for cancelling the rest of the Visconti tour, but I need to go back to the studio."

"No problem. I certainly understand."

As they drove back to Milan, he said, "Sorry about my past catching up with me and imposing additional demands on you."

The wind blew her hair around her face.

The noise level prevented them from conversing.

Alone with her thoughts, Cassandra hoped the network would make a decision in his show's favor and override Jared's fear of a cosmic justice winning out.

Chapter Nine

IX
The Hermit

Upon her return to New York City, Cassandra sat at the pretty hotel room desk, stared at her computer screen, and visited research sites. Without concentrating on what she read, she neither absorbed nor comprehended information.

Her mind kept drifting from tarot to Jared's sister, Sue. Her tragic life understandably had a negative effect on Jared. Cassandra wished she had the ability to comfort him. Lacking the skills of a therapist or theologian, she felt powerless.

She picked up the tarot card labeled IX, the Hermit. Regardless of the number of people in the city, alone in her hotel suite she felt isolated. Perhaps like the Hermit, stranded from her usual setting she could discover spiritual enlightenment.

Hard as she tried, she wasn't able to clear her mind.

Too distracted by thoughts of Sue, Cassandra typed in the name, Susan Ashbel. A link to a police blotter popped up.

Cassandra clicked it and read, *Susan Carolyn Ashbel arrested, for driving under the influence and possession of illegal substances, held in Kings County Detention Complex, is awaiting arraignment.*

Kings County was New York City's borough of Brooklyn.

She remembered Jared mentioning Sue had moved to Brooklyn.

Cassandra considered calling him to tell him about her discovery. If this Susan Ashbel was his sister he'd certainly want to post her bail.

However, if it wasn't the right Susan, he might be angry about Cassandra trying to stick her nose in his family's business.

She decided, before contacting him, she'd check out the woman's identity. She read the correction department's webpage.

She glanced at her watch. Taking the subway, she could be there in time for today's visiting hour.

She picked up The Hermit tarot card and slipped it into her jeans' pocket.

No matter how irrational, she headed out to visit Sue.

During the subway ride, anxiety stirred within Cassandra. She had no right to visit Jared's sister. She wasn't a family member or friend.

To calm her uneasiness she pulled out the tenth Major Arcana and peered at it.

If in custody, perhaps like the Hermit, solitude from Sue's familiar world could lead her to God's path. The card indicated, ideally, by being detached from external influences healing can begin.

Of course, there was nothing ideal about being in jail.

At the detention center, after passing the electronic security screening, Cassandra presented her ID to a police officer.

He handed her a list of rules. "Read and sign this."

She followed his instructions.

He signaled her to enter a glass-enclosed vestibule. "Take a seat in the next room."

After the officer buzzed her through two sets of doors, she glanced around an expansive area. With various sized formica topped tables and metal chairs, it resembled an institutional dining room.

There were a few people sitting, staring in space, and waiting.

She took a seat at a small round table.

Following three shrill sounds, a door at the far end of the room opened.

Four officers escorted five orange clad women into the space.

Within seconds, the visitors and four inmates met each other. Without touching, a few looked teary eyed.

Nervously, Cassandra approached the one woman who hadn't moved. She had stringy gray hair, and dark eyes, but her resemblance to Jared was unmistakable.

"Hi, Sue. You don't know me, but I've heard great things about you from your brother."

The woman squinted.

"Did Jared send you?"

"No. Could we sit and talk?"

"Sure. I have no place else to go."

Together they made their way to the small round table.

Cassandra blurted, "My name is Cassandra. Jared told me about your childhood. He really loves and cares about you."

Sue lowered her head. "Does he know about my arrest?"

"I don't think so."

"Then why are you here?"

"This is going to sound weird coming from a stranger, but I felt I should tell you, despite the chaos in your home, your brother cherishes the attention you gave him."

"Did you know we're only eleven months apart and were always real close. He was a great kid, is a swell man. I'm real proud of him. Wherever I've been, even in this awful place, I've tried to catch his shows." She rolled her eyes. "I still don't get what you're doing here. How do you know my brother?"

"Jared hired me to research a segment of *Fact or Truth*."

"What's it about?"

"The original meaning of tarot."

Sue's head jerked back. "Everyone knows they're fortunetelling cards."

"The first decks weren't used for that purpose. The first decks had religious significance."

"That's hard to believe."

Cassandra reached in her pocket for the tenth Arcana. She gave the card to Sue. "This card is called the Hermit."

She watched as Sue looked at the image of an elderly man carrying a walking stick in one hand and an hourglass in the other. "Who's the old guy?"

"He symbolizes all pilgrims who travel through time hoping to discover the right path of existence."

"As if there is one."

Cassandra kept interpreting the card. "In solitude, detached from everyday pressures, a person can reflect on what's important."

Sue laughed, "Sounds like me tucked away in a cell all by myself. Hey, I already know what's important. I need to get out of this joint."

"It must be hard to be away from home."

She didn't comment, but kept staring at the card. After a few minutes, Sue said, "Now that I'm through detox, other than to think I don't have much else to do."

Cassandra couldn't believe her audacity in asking, "What do you think about?"

Sue didn't answer.

Cassandra apologized. "Sorry. I didn't mean to pry."

Her tone softened, "It's okay. I've been thinking about my mom, my dad, the drugs, men... I don't know... all of it I guess."

"From what Jared told me, you were an innocent child."

"Really?" Sue looked into Cassandra's eyes. "I'll clue you in. I was far from innocent. I caused my parents a heap of trouble and I really hurt Jared."

Since she was privy to private information about Sue, Cassandra felt it fair to tell her, "When I was growing up, I thought I had the power to stop my mother from her obsessive worrying. I played the role of the quiet, good kid in an attempt to calm her down."

"Did it work?"

"Absolutely not. I didn't, still don't, have that kind of power."

"So you think I took the part of the bad kid to make my mom act normal? Is that your point?"

"Yes. And like me, no matter how you behaved you didn't have the power to change your mom."

"That's for sure. Yet that doesn't excuse the terrible things I've done."

"Why do you keep punishing yourself?"

"Is that's what you think I've been doing?"

"I think you keep punishing the innocent young Sue even though she, like any child, was powerless to change anyone especially a parent."

Sue stood up and raised her voice, "You know nothing about me, nothing about my depraved life. I walked the streets and turned tricks. I stole, lied, and did just about anything for a fix."

Cassandra hoped Sue wouldn't bolt.

Although Cassandra had no right to give advice, she tried to keep her voice steady. "I know when you forgive yourself the best of you, the real you, will come through."

Sue snickered, sat down, and crossed her arms over her chest. "Wouldn't it be better to forgive my mom? Not that I blame her for how she treated me, she was mentally ill, and couldn't stop herself."

"Didn't she stop herself by taking her life?"

Sue snapped, "Finding her dead body almost killed Jared."

Cassandra didn't know where her words were coming from. "Did any good come from her horrific act?"

Sue looked up at Cassandra. "I really haven't thought along those lines." She lowered her eyes.

The two women sat in silence.

Sue raised her head and made eye contact with Cassandra. "I guess the one good thing about her death was she no longer could directly inflict pain on anyone."

Tears streamed down her face. "Maybe she killed herself out of love."

"Although an irrational act, I think she took her life to protect the people she loved, you, Jared, and your dad."

"Maybe. It would be nice if Jared could see her death in that light."

"Maybe you could help him."

"Me? I can't even help myself."

"Have you tried to help Jared?"

"Yeah. I told him to stay away from me."

"Have you tried to help anyone else?"

"Like who?"

"I don't know. Maybe you could help kids get off drugs."

"Are you crazy? When I get out of here, I'll probably go back to using."

"Or you might not."

"I'm not sure I have the strength to..."

"Be yourself, to stay clean and sober, to help others?"

"Yeah. All that."

"I can relate."

Sue rolled her eyes.

Cassandra confessed, "Seriously, all my life I was timid and frightened. I allowed silly fears to inhibit the real me. I negated the fact God was and is always with me."

"You? You seem so… confident… so secure... so spiritual."

"I used to look frumpy. Rather than trusting God, I felt anxious, and was very shy. To be a member of your brother's TV cast his team gave me a makeover. At first, I tried to playact being self-assured, but once I started reaching out to others, sharing my thoughts, and presenting possible alternatives to their perspectives my self-esteem went up a few notches. I'll admit I've relied on the Lord to inspire me, to give me the right words to say at just the right moments. Perhaps, a similar game plan will work for you?"

Sue discreetly slipped her hand under the table and gave Cassandra's hand a squeeze. "Hey whoever you are, thanks for coming."

Three tones signaled the end of their visiting time.

"Fast hour."

Cassandra wanted to hug Sue. She didn't because it was against the rules. "Can I come see you again?"

"Sure. Anytime."

Cassandra remembered the visitation schedule indicated she could visit Sue in a few days, but didn't want to make a promise she might not be able to keep.

As Sue walked toward the door, she shouted over her shoulder, "Don't tell my brother about me being here."

On her way back to Manhattan, Cassandra hoped she wouldn't hear from Jared at least until she visited Sue again. She didn't think she would be able to stop herself from telling him about meeting his sister.

Within the confines of her hotel room, she focused on research to divert her attention from the both Jared and Sue.

The sound of the phone ringing caused her to jump.

She picked up the receiver and heard Jared's voice ask, "Are you free for dinner?"

Wanting to avoid seeing him she said, "I have to catch up with my work."

"As your boss, I insist you attend a dinner meeting."

Two hours later, she sat across from him in an Italian bistro.

He lifted a glass of red wine. "To a future trip to Italy."

After taking a few sips, he said, "I can't thank you enough for the wonderful time I had in Milan and isolating myself from the studio gave me time to think."

She looked at him expectantly.

He added, "Don't want to talk about network stuff, except for today's tarot card."

He tilted his head to the side indicating he was listening.

Feeling guilty for not mentioning her visit with Sue, Cassandra cleared her throat. "It's the tenth trump, called the Hermit."

"Tell me about it."

She described its image. "Like each of us, he's on a journey of self discovery."

Jared reached for her hands. "I'm grateful you visited my sister."

"How'd you know?"

"Sue called. Although she didn't allow me to get her released, she's willing to meet with one of my attorneys."

"That's fantastic."

Jared squeezed her fingertips, "She told me sometime in the future, when she's in a better mental place, she'd like to become a drug counselor."

"I'm happy for her, for you."

"I want to be hopeful. Yet, I fear her days of using drugs aren't over. Plans and promises from an addict aren't very reliable. What do you think?"

"It'll undoubtedly be a hard, uphill battle, but she's an insightful person."

"She sure is. I haven't heard her sound like my wise sister in a really long time. She told me, you helped her look at her relationship with our mom in a different way."

Cassandra pressed his palms. "And you? What are you feeling?"

His voice was intense and filled with raw emotion. "I've carried an ugly, darkness with me. I chose a fast pace hoping to avoid examining myself. I now know, I can't outrun me.

"But first, I have practical matters to attend to. I'm at a crossroads in my career and feel confused."

"I trust you'll figure things out."

"If you knew more about me you might not think so."

In that moment, Cassandra admitted to herself, she knew Jared was the man she loved.

Chapter Ten

X
The Wheel of Fortune

Early next morning, Cassandra received a disturbing text:

Give up your research. We've already done ours. We know where to find you.

Her immediate reaction was fear.

She took a deep breath and counted to ten. She reminded herself, unlike the old Cassie who was quick to retreat into a shell, her recently discovered self wouldn't allow the possibility of danger make her hide. She wouldn't allow herself to be enslaved by irrational emotions. Cassandra would rely on reason as her guide.

She thought of St. Aquinas' words, 'A man has free choice to the extent that he is rational.'

She chose to be logical. Perhaps, someone at the TV station was trying to sabotage Jared's series by frightening her. Thinking the text message was the work of a poor misguided soul, she dismissed the incident.

She switched her attention to researching the eleventh trump labeled X, The Wheel of Fortune. In its center was a blindfolded woman ready to turn an encircling wheel.

Four figures spun with the wheel. The top one depicted with donkey ears, sat on a pedestal, and held a scroll inscribed with, '*Regno*, I resign.' The man to his left also had donkey ears. Words from his mouth read, '*Regnabo*, I will resign.' Opposite him was a figure, with a donkey's tail. His words read, '*Ragnavi*, I have reigned.' The wheel rested on an old man whose words read, '*Sum sine Regno*, I am without a kingdom.'

Cassandra listed symbolic interpretations.

The card represented the blind dominion of chance.

Circumstances, no matter how lofty, will always change.

All things, including life itself, are temporal.

An animal's intellect and a hunger for earthly conquests can't stop cyclical movements.

The card's warning was clear. Don't be blinded by ego. One achievement in life is not enough to define a worthwhile existence. Don't allow the base instinct of laziness, one of the Seven Capital Sins, to direct you.

After several hours of reading, Cassandra decided to leave the hotel, get a quick lunch, and take the subway to her apartment. She wanted to pick up a book she had forgotten to pack. It contained photographs and interpretations of several old tarot decks.

During the subway ride, she thought about the Wheel of Fortune card. It was impossible for anyone to stay the same. By doing nothing, a person falls backward.

Applying this principle to her situation, she conjectured if she hadn't accepted Jared's offer to research tarot, she could've lost her chance for a raise or worse still she may have been fired.

While walking the few short blocks to her building, she put her hand in her pocket, felt the glossy tarot card, and wondered what the next turn of the wheel of fortune had in store for her.

Peering at the elaborate wrought iron scrollwork, she unlocked the front door. As she climbed the worn stairs, she felt a strange sensation. At the landing, she glanced up and down the quiet, empty hallway.

The slight pressure of putting her key into the keyhole caused her apartment door to swing wide open. To her horror, she gazed at a ransacked mess. Red liquid streaked the rug, and toppled furnishings. Due to a breeze coming from open windows, strewn book pages flew about.

Written in red letters, on the now cracked antique mirror above her fireplace was the word *STOP*.

She turned, ran down the stairs, and into the street.

She retrieved her cell phone from her purse and noticed she had received another text.

The devil knows all. He doesn't like people trampling his toes. Stop your research or else you'll be sorry.

Rather than feeling frightened, Cassandra felt incensed. Someone had invaded her home, violated her privacy, and was trying to control her.

She tapped the numbers 911.

"What's your emergency?"

She gave details to the dispatcher.

While she waited for the police to arrive, she called Jared, told him about the break-in, and read him the text messages.

He shared, "I've gotten all kinds of prank messages in the past. Some were quite nasty, but always harmless. Stay put, I'll be right there."

A squad car with blurring sirens, pulled up to the curb. Two police officers briefly introduced themselves before rushing into the building to check her apartment.

Following their direction, she stood next to their car.

Minutes later, a black sedan pulled up behind it. A man wearing a suit and tie introduced himself, "I'm Detective Gomez. Just a few questions ma'am while the team makes sure it's safe for you to enter your apartment."

Cassandra freely and honestly answered his questions. She also showed him the texts she received.

Jared arrived, ran to her, and introduced himself, "My name is Jared Ashbel. Dr. Visconti is conducting research for a segment of my television show."

The officer said, "Dr. Visconti told us about her work."

Silently Jared stood by her side until the interview was complete.

The officer concluded by saying, "Excuse me a minute while I check in with the officers." He spoke into a small, barely visible two-way radio attached to his lapel.

He turned to Cassandra. "Ma'am we need you to look around your place. Tell us if anything is missing, but first we need to dust for prints, take fiber and other samples.

"Ma'am, I must warn you, from the level of destruction, it appears we're dealing with a very angry person." The officer turned to Jared. "Do you know of anyone who would want to hurt Dr. Visconti?"

He shook his head.

"Is there someone who would like to stop the television segment from going forward?"

"Not even my biggest competitor would stoop this low."

"Are you sure?"

"Yes. I'm sure. There are easier, legitimate ways to damage the show's image. In fact, this incident might be newsworthy. If given a chance, the press could inadvertently give *Fact or Truth* free publicity and stir audience interest."

Cassandra wondered if Jared's statement led the officer to consider Jared a suspect.

"You two go for coffee. Dr. Visconti I'll call you, probably in a couple of hours, when you can visit the crime scene."

She faced Jared, "There's a café down the street."

He put his arm around her shoulders.

His touch replaced angst with desire.

In the cozy setting, they sat across from each other.

He ordered a burger, fries, and a chocolate shake.

She ordered a pot of chamomile tea.

"How's Sue?"

"Her attorney believes, because it's her first arrest, the judge might be lenient. He hopes to settle the case quickly."

"Did you see her?"

"I was on my way back from the county jail when you called."

"Has she agreed to be released on bail?"

"No. Not yet. She feels she deserves to be there. She said something about needing to take responsibility for her actions."

"And maybe she feels it's safer to be among criminals than alone with the temptations on the street."

He shrugged his shoulders. "Years ago I accepted losing her. Seeing her, hearing her rational words felt like a gift. It was as if she had risen from the dead reincarnated as the real Sue."

"I'm happy for both of you. Would it be okay for me to visit her?"

"Maybe in a few days. Seems she wants to be by herself for now." He abruptly changed the subject. "Why don't you stay at my place? It's big enough for you to have your own space and I promise not to intrude on your privacy."

Cassandra pondered, *Was her newfound freedom about to end?*

"I feel perfectly safe at the hotel, but I hate to have the network keep paying my expenses."

"Don't worry about the cost. The studio rents the suite on a regular basis whether it's occupied or not."

As she lifted the steaming brew to her lips, she felt his eyes focus on her shaky hands.

"What card are you currently researching?"

"The eleventh trump, The Wheel of Fortune."

"From its name I guess it means life's unpredictable."

"Indeed, life can quickly change."

"Like my business, one minute you're nobody, next you're the star ready to fall. Fame and fortune are fleeting."

"As is everything."

"Yeah, my dad would like to quote the second line from Ecclesiastics, 'Vanity of vanity. Everything is vanity.' In other words, everything is meaningless."

"Except for our souls. Whether rich or poor anyone can detach from the wheel of fortune to achieve spiritual success."

"How so?"

"There's one part of a wheel that doesn't turn.

"Its axis?"

She nodded. "God is a constant and stable force in our lives. While events are unpredictable God has a purposeful plan for each of us."

"So we have no control?"

"By using our intellect we can follow His plan regardless of what happens."

"I'm confused. If He has a plan won't it play out no matter what we do?"

"It's not that straight forward."

Her cell rang. Rather than continuing to answer Jared, she answered the call.

"Yes Detective, I'll be right there."

Jared said, "I'd like to come with you."

"Thank you. I might need a shoulder to cry on."

She walked at a quick pace. "I'd like to get this over with as soon as possible."

Detective Gomez met them at the entrance of the building. "Before you go up to your apartment you should know someone spattered blood on your belongings. I'm afraid most are ruined. There was an animal's heart in your otherwise empty refrigerator."

Her eyes widened, "Blood? I thought it was red paint." As the magnitude and vile nature of her violation began to register in her mind, she felt her head spinning and her knees buckling.

As her body swayed, Jared laced his arm around her waist, held her upright, and prevented her from falling. "Detective, is it really necessary for Cassandra to go upstairs?"

"I'm afraid so. She's the only one who would know if something is missing."

She took a deep breath and stepped out of his reach. "It's okay. I feel better now."

Following the detective, they slowly climbed the steps to her apartment. She held onto the banister with one hand. Jared held her other hand.

Despite the gloomy situation, Cassandra felt a titillating excitement emanating from his strong grip. The sensation spread through her body and reduced her nervousness, at least, for the moment.

The detective opened the door and held up the yellow tape cordoning off her home.

She paused at the threshold, let go of Jared's hand, and stepped in front of him. Although he placed his hands on her shoulders, she felt a cold current assault her. She internally trembled.

Without going too far into the room, she peered at the debris. She craned her neck, but failed to see any pieces of furniture intact.

Words accompanied by tears slipped out. "Why would someone go to such lengths to destroy my things?" Her shivering became noticeable.

Jared wrapped his arms around her. "It's as if he knew just how to get to you."

"What could someone hope to gain from frightening me?"

"You're more important to the show than you think."

"Or maybe it's more personal?"

Detective Gomez asked, "What makes you think so?"

"It hurts so much to see…" She took a few deep breaths in order to prevent herself from sobbing. "My things weren't worth much money, but because people I love gave them to me they were priceless and irreplaceable."

Jared asked, "I hope this senseless act doesn't convince you to quit the show?"

She moved away from his touch, turned, and faced him. "This act of vandalism makes me more determined than ever to complete my research. However, I don't understand why eliminating me from the segment would matter. The show would go on with or without me."

"Because what's obvious to everyone, and what you're blind to is I care about you. I'd go as far as canceling the segment to protect you."

Feeling somewhat dizzy, although she heard his words, she couldn't quite sort out their meaning. Did he care about her as a colleague, a friend, the person who he perceived helped his sister, or as a woman?

"More than ever, I feel compelled to defend the spiritual nature of tarot. Religious people have as much right to hear the truth regardless of how loud occultists shout falsehoods."

By clearing his throat, the detective redirected Cassandra's attention.

She stepped between rubble.

As she fingered broken objects tears flowed down her cheeks.

As she entered her bedroom, the level of destruction seemed to increase. Her clothes slashed to shreds covered the floor. Her bare mattress had gashes across its foam top surface. On the wall, the words NO TAROT were written in blood and had pages from a book stuck to them.

The detective pointed. "Do you recognize any of these pages?"

She walked closer and examined two or three. Chills raced down her spine. "They're from a book about tarot. It's the book I wanted to pick up today to help me with my research."

A pungent odor, emanating from the dried blood, made her nauseous.

She dashed toward the bathroom, and heard the detective yell, "Don't go in there."

Although she stopped short, she saw a naked blowup doll wearing a curly brown wig sprawled out on the floor. Blood dripped from its face trailing to where she stood.

Then her mind went blank.

Chapter Eleven

XI
Strength

Feeling comfortable and safe, Cassandra awakened ensconced in Jared's arms.

She glanced around and realized she was in the back seat of a police car. "What happened?"

Jared told her, "You fainted, but you're all right now."

She felt the car move. "Where're we going?"

"To my place."

She wriggled out of his embrace. "No. I want to go to the hotel." She raised her voice, "Officer, please drive to the Plaza."

"Yes, ma'am."

Jared objected, "But you shouldn't be alone."

"I think being alone is exactly what I need."

At the hotel, he escorted her to her suite. "Sure you don't want company?"

"Yes. I'm sure. I want to shower and change into clean clothes."

"I'll call you later."

"Thank you for being with me today."

She gently closed the door and slithered to the floor. Her body heaved and released sobs she had managed to suppress for most of the day. Minutes turned into an hour before she felt utterly drained. After cleaning up, she crawled into bed.

She spent subsequent hours twisting and turning, her mind frequently replaying the morbid scene she spied in her bathroom.

The ringing of her cell startled her.

She bolted straight up and reached for her phone.

Jared's voice filled with concern asked, "How you doing?"

"Resting."

"Think you're up for a drive in the country tomorrow?"

She hesitated.

"It'll do you good. I'll pick you up at nine."

Having an outing with Jared to look forward to helped Cassandra relax and get the rest she desperately needed.

The morning sunlight filled her room. Stretching her arms over her head, she realized she had slept soundly. With enthusiasm, she showered and dressed.

Along the Plaza's circle drive, Jared waited for her. He seemed content sitting behind the wheel of a green Corvette,

He cheerfully welcomed her, "Good morning."

She returned his greeting and sat in the passenger seat. "Is this one yours?" she asked.

"For the day it is."

Once out of the city, they stopped at a bakery for coffee and pastries.

"My guess is you studied a tarot card before leaving the hotel. Am I right?"

She giggled. "You're growing a white beard." She reached over the small table and dusted powdered sugar off his cheeks. "Want to hear about the twelfth Arcana?"

"Absolutely."

"It's called Strength."

"How timely."

Without asking whom he thought needed courage, she described the card. "In the Visconti-Sforza deck it portrays a man holding a stick over a cowering lion. You might wonder why the lion is afraid. Did the man represent the good side of humanity and the lion base animal instincts? Was goodness stronger than evil?

"The Rider-Waite's Strength card had an image of a young woman dressed in white decorated with flowers. Her left hand is over a lion's nose and her right hand is under its chin. The lion's tongue extended from its mouth makes him look helpless, but he has the ability to avoid pain by pulling his tongue back in his mouth. Looking at this card, one could wonder if gentleness is more powerful than brashness."

"Isn't strength one of the four cardinal virtues in *Plato's Republic*?"

"Yes. In his view, it represents man's victory over the violent forces of nature. It symbolizes man's determination of will to impose personal limits on excessive cravings."

"Plato's advice, of course, is to do all things in moderation."

She nodded in agreement. "The path to coming to terms with existential struggles lies in choosing to renounce certain vanities and vices. Cruel people, like Filippo Visconti, misused power. He was an angry tyrant. Dissatisfied with his appearance, he was a weak coward who chose to victimize others. Ironically, his lack of moral strength, not only wounded those he encountered, but rendered him cursed with the embodiment of true ugliness."

As they headed toward Connecticut, Cassandra assumed they'd be going to the Yale University Library in New Haven to view the Cary Collection of Playing Cards. These cards, also known as the Visconti di Modrone tarot deck, dated back to around 1466. She anticipated viewing the only historical western deck with six ranks of face cards and trumps containing the three theological virtues of faith, hope, and charity.

She asked Jared, "How's Sue? With your permission, I'd like to visit her."

"Forgot to tell you. The judge released her. She's in a halfway house and can't have visitors for a while."

Her cell rang. Glancing at it, she told Jared, "It's Detective Gomez."

From the tone of the detective's voice, Cassandra felt he was anxious to close the case. "Dr. Visconti forensics collected evidence from your apartment. You're free to have it cleaned. I'll text you a few numbers you can call to make the necessary arrangements."

"Thank you. Any leads on who invaded my space and destroyed my things?"

His indirect answer was, "It may take time to apprehend the person responsible."

Relieved she wouldn't have to see the awful mess again, she immediately called an agency that specialized in cleaning crime scenes. She turned to Jared. "I spoke to my landlord last night. Fortunately, he took the incident well and gave me permission to have my apartment painted."

Absorbed in her recent calls she was surprised to see Jared turning onto her parents' street.

"Where're you going?"

"Forgive me for being forward. I called your parents last night and asked if we could stop by. I figured you might want to tell them, in person, about what happened at your place. I also thought you'd like a friend at your side when you filled them in on the details."

With each of her heartbeats, her level of dread increased. "Thank you for doing something I was trying to avoid. I know it's best for them to hear about the incident from me, but I don't know how I'll be able to convince them I've decided not to quit my research."

He pulled into their driveway. "Don't worry."

While they approached the entrance to her parents' home, she said a silent prayer asking God for strength.

Her mother and father greeted them, hugging Cassandra and shaking hands with Jared.

The pair followed her parents into the sunroom.

"What a delightful space," Jared said.

Cassandra told him, "It's my favorite part of the house."

Her mother asked, "Would you like tea, coffee, or juice? Are you hungry?"

Jared politely answered, "Nothing, thank you. We just had a bite to eat."

With her parents sitting on chairs opposite their visitors they took turns in asking Jared general questions about his life.

Cassandra tried to stop their interrogation, but Jared insisted, "Having nothing to hide, I don't mind your parents' inquires. And I can appreciate their interest in knowing something about the man you're working with."

Her parents shifted their attention to his TV show. Her father asked, "I don't understand the title of your series. It's called *Fact or Truth* isn't it? Don't facts and truth mean the same thing?"

Jared explained, "Remember the children's story of the three blind men and an elephant. Each man felt a different part of the animal. Each man came to a different conclusion regarding what type of animal it was. We, too, can be deluded by focusing on partial viewpoints, although each contains facts. We need to see the whole picture to know what really is.

"Sometimes it takes many facts to uncover the truth. Sometimes, facts can mislead us into making false conclusions. They can be contradictory. While facts can answer why questions of how, where, or what, they may not spell out the entire truth. We can acknowledge facts, but we have to seek the truth. And in a theological sense, regardless of a lack of facts, God's truth is absolute."

"Amen." Her mother's tone was clear and steady.

Cassandra worried he may have confused the issue by pointing out facts can exist in reality while truths can be things that one believes to be true and can be subjective.

She thought of notes and lyrics from a songbook being facts, but knew truth came from performers singing from their hearts.

She thought of a skyscraper's blueprint providing exact engineering specifications or facts, but only with construction completed would the truth of its design become apparent.

She thought of the many facts regarding the ocean's unending movement, but truth was, without watching its waves, experiencing its wetness, and feeling its power suck her from the shore she couldn't fully appreciate its true essence.

Her mother's voice interrupted Cassandra's thoughts. "I'll be frank. Without being a family man, this may be hard for you to comprehend, but the truth is we're strongly opposed to our daughter working for you. We feel by dabbling into the occult she's risking her soul. You need to know, she was raised to fear God not to defy Him."

"Mom, we didn't come here to be lectured."

Her father piped up, "Jared, last night you mentioned on the phone about wanting to tell us something."

Cassandra prefaced her comments. "Please hear me out before you react." She proceeded to tell them about her vandalized apartment.

Her mother reached for her father's hand. Her horrified look spoke louder than her words, "Cassie, you must, I repeat you must end your assignment and quit your job. With your experience, you'll soon find a new position in your field.

"You must stay here with us so you can be far from the terrible big city.

"Father Jorge will hear your confession. You can tell him all about your involvement with the occult and beg him to give you absolution for your sins."

"Mom and Dad, I know you mean well, but I choose not to leave the show."

"But you must end your tarot research before the awful man who destroyed your things harms you." Her mother mopped her wet eyes with a lacy handkerchief. "Aren't you terrified of him?"

Cassandra shook her head. "Rather than being afraid of the person who did this, I feel sorry for him."

Her mother reached out and squeezed Cassandra's arm. "You're obviously too distraught to be thinking straight. From the way you're dressed, in those tight pants and flimsy blouse, I can see you're under some kind of spell."

Cassandra patiently patted her mother's hand. "I can only imagine a wounded soul filled with fear and rage would have done this senseless act. Only a frustrated individual could have tried to frighten me."

"But he can kill you."

Cassandra said, "From what my faith in God has taught me, I want to look beyond these vile acts. I want to forgive my brother in Christ."

Her father said, "While forgiving, you need to protect yourself from this dangerous person. I have to agree with your mother. I won't let anyone endanger you. We insist on you staying here under our protection until after Mr. Ashbel's shows airs." He tilted his head toward Jared, "And we demand Mr. Ashbel, you not associate our daughter's name with any aspect of your TV show."

Thinking of the Strength tarot card, she recalled the image of the lion. It reminded her she had the ability to remain quiet. Instead, she opened her mouth and tried in vain to explain her feelings, "Dad, besides losing things dear to me, I don't want to further injure myself. I can't undo what this stranger has done and I'm not delusional. I realize I have no control over him, but I won't let him terrify me." She felt victorious. "I'm not a victim. I won't become a slave to fear."

"But…" her mother began.

Cassandra cut her off with a lesson she learned earlier from the twelfth tarot card. "It takes more strength to create than to destroy. In this case, it probably took the vandal mere hours to destroy precious heirlooms crafted by skilled carpenters and craftsmen. And it'll take a long time for me to make my apartment a home again."

Jared elaborated, "That's because it's harder to do good than it is to do evil."

Her mother said, "You're talking philosophical gibberish instead of being practical."

Cassandra responded, "Practically speaking, I want to help Jared create a segment accurately telling the truth about tarot cards. My aim is simply to present historical facts to dispel illusions and inordinate fears. The cards created as a parlor game give a path to spiritual enlightenment, a path to our Devine Savior, Jesus Christ.

"I would think being a Visconti you each would like the world to know the facts, good and bad, about your ancestors. I'd think you'd like people to know the truth about the Visconti-Sforza tarot deck."

She rose, moved closer to her parents, and took one of each of their hands in hers. "Please, Mom and Dad give me a chance to be better than the poor soul who injured me. Let me live our faith."

Her father dismissed her by saying, "I'll say good-bye to you and your boss. Being it's my day off, I have yard work waiting for me."

Her mother closed her eyes and melodramatically recited, "God save you my child."

In the quiet car ride back to New York City, Cassandra told Jared, "I'm sorry you had to witness my parents' overprotective side. They're really good people who I greatly injured."

"Want to hear my observations?" He didn't wait for her to reply. "I was surprised by your parents' coldness. Until an hour ago, I envied your childhood, but today I pitied you. You've tried so hard to appease and please your folks. In my opinion, they aren't capable of appreciating your goodness. They seem to measure love out in quantifiable installments. By making judgments based on rigid rules rather than reality, they've missed the beauty of you, their precious child. I saw your parents, similar to mine, caught up in themselves."

She felt he was exaggerating and transferring his ill feelings from his father onto her parents.

He took in a deep breath. "And it was good for me to see too much attention, while perhaps not as destructive as too little, isn't a good thing either." He softened his tone, "However, in the end I can agree with your assessment. Our parents came from loving, albeit, distorted places of love. Guess in their own ways our mothers and fathers did their best."

As if having an afterthought he asked, "Does your parents' dogmatic approach to life shake your faith?"

Confused by his riveting words, rather than answering his question or responding to his opinion directly, she asked, "When was the last time you spoke to your dad?"

With his eyes focusing on the road, he said, "Too long, I guess."

"Do you think he'd like to hear about Sue's path to recovery?"

He didn't answer, but she thought she knew Jared well enough to assume he'd think about reaching out to his father.

Chapter Twelve

XII
The Hanged Man

Time went by without Cassandra hearing from Detective Gomez. Like most minor crimes in the city, she assumed the police didn't consider vandalizing her apartment a top priority. Therefore, she was surprised to receive the detective's call. "We've apprehended the men who invaded your apartment."

She automatically asked, "Who are they?"

"We think it best you come down to the station. I suggest you wait until you get here before calling anyone."

"Are you sure you have the right men."

"They confessed."

"Why did they choose my home?"

"I need to speak to you in person. Since I'll be tied up all morning, could you stop by after one?"

While waiting for the hours to pass, although hard to concentrate on working, Cassandra researched the thirteenth Major Arcana, XII, The Hanged Man.

She read the card had controversial interpretations including ones referring to it as the traitor, Judas. It could represent betraying faith. It could represent judicial torture and the ultimate punishment of lacking spiritualism.

Her mind shifted to thoughts of Jared's disillusionment with his spiritual beliefs. He felt disconnected from his father and the senior man's view of Christianity.

Rather than listening to his children's feelings, offering them personal comfort, helping them understand their mother, and aid them in coping with the confusion in their fractured home, Jared's father hid behind a wall of biblical quotes.

In his young mind, Jared linked his father and the Bible together. Over the years, Jared felt both his father and the Bible failed in protecting and supporting his sister, Sue.

Cassandra wished she could help Jared tease out the good in his childhood, but his anger overshadowed his perspective.

She thought of his remarks regarding her parents. In part, he was correct. In the past, to gain their approval, she hid her true feelings and acted as they expected her to.

However, she couldn't believe her parents weren't capable of loving her unconditionally. She felt certain, given enough time they'd accept her position regarding her tarot research.

However, if Jared's appraisal of her parents proved to be true, Cassandra hoped her faith wouldn't be shaken.

Hours later, Cassandra entered Detective Gomez's office.

"I hope you're strong enough to hear this?"

A bolt of anxiety made her tremble.

"The intruders were Felix Barnes and Joe Korsky. Do you recognize their names?"

Cassandra thought for a few minutes. "No. I don't think I've ever heard of them."

"Barnes is a two bit actor down on his luck. He's living with relatives in Hartford. Korsky is a bouncer at a rundown bar near Felix's temporary residence. We lifted his prints from your apartment. He had a few priors for assault and battery. While interrogating him, in an effort to plea bargain, he ratted on his friend Felix."

She tilted her head waiting for the detective to continue.

His next words hit her like a punch in her stomach. "Your father paid these men to vandalize your place."

Cassandra gagged and tried to hold back a wave of nausea.

The detective waited for her to accept his statement.

In an attempt to soothe her rattled nerves, denial came from her lips, "I don't believe these men. They must be lying."

"We've interrogated them separately and their stories match."

She tried relying on logic. "But you yourself said one's an actor He could've written a script they both memorized."

"They gave us dates and places where they met with your dad."

"What does that prove?"

"It was enough to confront your father."

Her emotions kept shifting. She felt enraged. "I can't believe you bothered him with this nonsense. Do these men... Barnes and Korsky believe in the occult? Are they some kind of fanatics?"

No matter her reaction, Detective Gomez maintained his polite tone. "I'd like you to listen to a recording."

Preparing to hear the men confess, Cassandra rested her elbows on the arms of the chair.

When the detective pressed the play button, she heard her father identify himself. "Yes, I'm Mr. Antonio Visconti and I agree to be recorded."

She leaned her body forward and got closer to the small device.

"Guess you got me." There was a long pause. "I only paid the men to stage the threats in order to protect my little girl. I never meant for them to commit a crime. I'm completely responsible for the damages. You have to let the pair go."

She heard Detective Gomez ask, "Tell us why we should release Felix Barnes and Joe Korsky?"

Wanting to block out what she was hearing, she scooted her chair back from the desk, but her father's voice continued to reach her ears. "Ever since we learned of Cassie being snared into the occult's bottomless net, her mother and I have been sick worrying about our child's eternal soul. We prayed. We visited our church. We implored Cassie to stop researching tarot, but she wouldn't listen. Right before our eyes, we saw her fall into the hands of the devil. She changed her hairstyle, she dressed like a harlot, and she sassed us. We had to do something to stop her before it was too late. Her mother and I came up with the plan of terrorizing her. We felt it was for her own good to be shocked back to her faith."

He pressed the stop button. "Heard enough?"

Parlayed by disbelief she didn't respond.

"Your father is in the next room. Would you like a few minutes alone with him before pressing charges?"

Staring into space she whispered, "I won't be pressing charges. Please release him and his hired help."

With her world turned upside down, she felt like the hanged man. Her father's words equated to a reversal of everything she believed in, everything she knew about him, her mother, and herself.

Her foggy mind heard the detective's voice. "I'm going to get a cup of coffee? Would you like some?"

She robotically replied, "No, thank you."

He left her alone with her muddled thoughts and her jumbled emotions.

By the time he returned, she wanted to hear her father say something to help her accept his actions. "I'm ready to see my dad."

Detective Gomez escorted her down a brightly lit hallway to an integration room.

He knocked once, turned the knob, opened the door, and ushered her inside.

In the sterile space, her father was sitting on one side of a metal table. His hands folded, his head held high, and his eyes staring straight ahead.

She sat across from him and observed he appeared to be very tired and seemed to have aged since last she saw him.

Still standing by the entrance Detective Gomez said, "Mr. Visconti, since your daughter decided not to press charges, you're free to go." He left the room.

Cassandra waited for her father to speak. She expected him to sound nervous and offer an apology.

Instead, he ordered, "Let's get out of this dreadful place."

He pushed back his chair and started to rise, but her hands moved downward indicating she wanted him to wait a moment. "Why? Why did you hire those men to destroy my beautiful treasures?"

Void of affect, he spoke in his usual monotone voice. "I only did it to protect you. We couldn't stand by while that wretched TV man manipulated you." His detached expression seemed to mock his words. "Because your mother and I love you so much, we did what was necessary to put you back on the Lord's path. Someday you'll thank us for saving your soul from the devil."

She shuddered. Were her parents like Adam and Eve? Did her parents' egos grow so huge they assumed they could define love better than the Holy Scriptures did? Controlled by their emotions, fear had led them to commit criminal behaviors. She wondered when they had switched from worshiping the Creator to worshiping a created version of their religious teachings.

She pitied them for not recognizing their arrogance. "Perhaps, speaking to Father Jorge will help you understand what you've done. From all you've taught me I know our church offers peace, hope, and love not prejudice, fear, and hate. I'm sure our pastor will be able to help you with your guilt."

His head jerked back. "I have no regrets."

Feeling sorry for his lack of atonement, she stood, walked out of the room, through the long hallway, and out the front door of the police station.

She ran down the subway stairs and dashed between closing doors of a crowded car. She grabbed onto a pole. As the train rumbled over the tracks, her body swayed and her mind raced. She thought of the Hangman tarot card. By genuinely forgiving her parents, she could grow closer to living one with God, but she wasn't sure if she was strong enough to let go of her rage.

Suddenly, she had a deeper understanding of how Jared felt toward his father. Earlier she wanted to help Jared focus on the joys he experienced in childhood. Now her mind felt crowded with memories of her parents shoving their questionable beliefs down her throat. She seethed with disgust for their misguided zeal. Today's revelations took her beyond anything she'd known or imaged. A profound ache darkened her spirits. Her parents' negative views, like a deep abyss, made her feel she couldn't reach them. Their decisions, their actions alienated her from them. She felt like an orphan.

In her youth, her parents tied her to them with invisible strings. As she grew, the strings tightened making it uncomfortable for her to grow. Rather than cutting the strings, out of fear of losing their approval, she chose to remain entwined in their stifling bondage.

Recently, magicians changed her outward appearance. With her new image, she gained enough confidence to start unraveling the strangulating strings around her heart. In the police station, having learned of her parents' actions, she felt a severing of the last string binding her to them. Their extreme measures left her no other choice, but to give up her dependence on them.

It was as if her childhood had ended.

But, was she finally free to be an independent woman?

As a true follower of her faith, she wanted to focus on love and forgiveness. She wanted to gain understanding rather than feeling hounded by a sense of betrayal. She wanted to be capable of accepting her parents with their flaws and still love them, appreciate them, and for many reasons feel blessed to have had them raise her.

More than ever, she felt tarot research was part of God's plan for her to mature. Moving away from her parents emotionally opened a way for her inner self to emerge. She no longer was little Cassie. She no longer would enjoy working in a deafeningly quiet office space. She no longer would be comfortable wearing unflattering clothes. She no longer would be content to retreat into a shell of silence. And she would no longer be satisfied to hide her feelings in order to please others.

She prayed, "Please God let me switch from philosophical contemplations to putting my words into action, putting my beliefs into practice, I want to find your truth and be called to a higher purpose where I can accept not my will, but your will."

Chapter Thirteen

XIII
Death

With mixed emotions, Cassandra entered the Plaza's lobby. To her surprise, Jared turned from the front deck and walked toward her.

She guessed Detective Gomez, thinking she needed a friend's support, called Jared.

As he approached, she noticed he looked pale. His eyes were bloodshot and puffy.

He asked, "Cassandra, can I come up to your suite?"

Assuming he knew what her parents had done she wondered, *Did he fear she'd quit working on the tarot segment or was he here to fire her?* Another thought crossed her mind. *Did the network cancel his Fact or Truth show?*

She nodded and walked with him to the elevator. His slumped shoulders and shuffling gait led her to believe something more important than any of these issues was troubling him.

Her concerns switched to anxiety.

In silence, they went up to the nineteenth floor.

Once inside her living room, he sat on the gray, tufted couch and stared into space.

She sat next to him. "What's wrong?"

He blurted, "Sue is dead."

Tears slipped from her eyes. A sharp pain sliced her heart, ripping it open. Minutes earlier, she foolishly grieved her lost childhood. Now, the hollow pang of real death felt unbearable.

The sound of Jared's voice acted as a reminder she needed to be there for him and help him absorb the shock of his loss.

"Early this morning, I was summoned to New York Hospital. Specialists explained two decades of drug use had weakened Sue's heart. Although she survived a massive heart attack, her heart sustained extensive damage. The doctors told me there was nothing they could do to save her.

"Sue was in critical condition. Yet she looked radiant. She embraced death with dignity and told me, 'I feel close to our Maker. I feel He'll welcome me home.' She said she could see Christ's light and knew her existence was just beginning."

Cassandra knelt on the gold tone area rug in front of Jared. She took his hands in hers.

He stared into her eyes. "As ugly as death is, I feel blessed. I had long since counted her as one of the departed. And God granted my wish of having a few more happy hours with my precious sister. Before He stopped her heart from beating, during those brief moments, it was as if I had the privilege of peering at her resurrected soul. She was at peace and filled with joy."

He slithered to the floor and kissed Cassandra on each cheek. "You led Sue to a healing path. For that, I'm infinitely grateful.

"And I can't begin to express my gratitude to you for suggesting I contact my dad. I left him a message. I told him I was no longer angry and hoped he'd be able to forgive me. I told him Sue had quit using drugs."

Jared sucked in his breath and slowly exhaled. "While I was holding onto the last of Sue's life, our dad called. I wasn't about to take any calls, but had to shut off the phone's ringer. When I glimpsed his face, I answered. He began apologizing to me and wanted desperately to speak to Sue. I told him we were together. I put the phone on speaker and heard him telling Sue how much he loved her. As weak as she was, she told him she loved him, too. She told us not to waste any more time living in the past."

Following a few silent moments, Jared said, "After her... I spoke to my dad again. Ironically, I mentioned something from my biblical teachings. Christ died to save us. We have to die to ourselves in order to save Christ within us. Our physical death enables us to live eternally with the Lord."

Tears slid down his cheeks and onto his shirt. "I'm confident Sue is cradled in Jesus' loving arms."

Cassandra thought about the people in her life. Her parents were undoubtedly religious and Father Jorge was definitely a holy man. As she felt Jared's warm breaths on her face, she realized although he wasn't religious and far from holy, despite his protestations, he was deeply spiritual.

He moved back a few inches and asked, "What does tarot say about death?"

Her mind shifted to her research. "In the Visconti-Sforza deck the Death card is a reminder of death's inevitability. Regardless of who we are, or what we possess on earth we will all die. Yet, rather than an ending, once we embrace death we can view it, as Sue did, as a beginning to enlightenment, understanding, and to eternal joy.

"The card also refers to the necessity, during everyone's lifetime, for aspects of personal existence to die in order for an individual to grow and live more fully."

His fingertips wiped away the tears skimming her cheeks. "Sue wouldn't want us to be unhappy."

Cassandra noticed he had stopped crying. She wanted to reassure him. "Similar to Sue's insights, tarot's Death card suggests the heart of truth is the light, Christ's light. His light leads us out of darkness to experience the fullness of life in the present, the future, and forever."

Chapter Fourteen

XIV
Temperance

As Jared was about to leave, he told Cassandra, "I've decided to make the long overdue trip to visit my dad. With him still living in my childhood home, you can image my apprehension."

While she hugged him, he said, "I hope during our mutual time of deep sorrow, we'll be able to share our love in mourning Sue."

He kissed her forehead before making a quick exit.

To avoid dwelling on her grief, she spent time researching the fifteenth Major Arcana labeled XIV, Temperance. Its image depicted a maiden pouring liquid from one vessel into another. Her action implied she, like a chemist, was in the process of creating a new mixture. Symbolically, it represented change of thought can occur by adding reflection to memories. Through repentance a positive transcendence can occur. Through insight, a person can achieve a different awareness and perceive events from a new perspective. Through discernment, we're able to identify reality. Through enlightenment, we're able to unite with God.

It also referred to balancing corporal desires with spiritual wisdom. Having a balance between satisfying physical wants and adhering to God's universal laws equated to a healthy life.

She thought of a rapist. He exemplified an unhealthy person who selfishly focused on satisfying violent urges. Regardless of why he was angry, he violated God's law of loving his neighbor as himself. In his narrow vision, he didn't consider his innocent victim's feelings and her right to make her own choices.

To some extent, perhaps not as blatantly, in order to satisfy certain impulses we all ignore God's laws. At these times, each of us experiences moments where we jeopardize our relationship with God.

Her thoughts kept coming back to Jared. She thought of him and his father. *Would the two men pour out their hurts and come to new conclusions? Through their sharing, could they recover from their past wounds? Would they express regrets for their spoken and unspoken words?*

Through spiritual conversion, Sue transformed her life from despair to hope. Would her father and brother do the same?

As mature adults, could Jared and his father master their irrational instincts and reach a place of harmony? Could they strike a balance of ideas and reach mutual understanding? Could they adopt healthier parameters? Could they create a new relationship or would they stay stuck in their past dysfunctional one?

Her mind shifted to her situation. Upset with her mother and father she wondered if it was possible for her to recover from their betrayal. To mitigate her negative energy, she realized she needed to add temperance to the seemingly endless stream of rage she felt toward them.

Of course in their eyes they were only doing what they felt was best for her. How could she blame them for doing what they'd always done? They had difficulty tempering their anxieties with their faith in her and in the Lord. Their egos seemed to get in the way of what they professed to believe in, namely trust in God.

As much as she despised their recent behaviors, her feelings for them hadn't changed. She picked up her cell and tapped in her mother's number. Her call went straight to voice mail. "Mom, I called to tell you I love you and Dad, too."

Later, when she didn't receive a call back, she assumed her parents weren't ready to speak to her. Maybe she, too, needed more time before sharing feelings.

Returning to her research, she studied the relationship between temperance and balance. Most raw impulses weren't good or bad in themselves. We simply needed to temper impulses with moderation. Fearing extreme consequences her parents often condemned sensible behaviors.

Cassandra realized she had lived a regimented existence. Absorbing her parents' worries, she had limited her growth. She didn't drive because she might be in a car accident. She didn't ski because she could break a leg. She didn't date, because a man could be unfaithful.

It was clear she needed to find a balance between work and pleasure. She thought of, 'For everything there is a season' (Ecclesiastes 3:1).

She strolled into the bedroom and gazed in the full-length mirror at her image. She smiled as she decided it was time to accept reality by feeling comfortable being an attractive woman, a desirable woman.

Her mood abruptly changed. Sue no longer had the opportunity to do earthy things like hugging her brother, talking to her father, or falling in love.

Overcome with sadness Cassandra sobbed.

Minutes later, she grabbed a tissue and stopped sniffling. She thought of Sue's wise advice to her family. She told her father and brother to go forward with their lives.

Cassandra could also benefit from this wisdom.

She again thought of a message from Ecclesiastes, 'A time to weep and a time to laugh, a time to mourn; and a time to dance (Ecclesiastes 3:4).

She thought of the last time she laughed. She was with Jared. On a hot humid day, to avoid going out in the sticky weather, he had ordered lunches for himself and Cassandra.

They sat at a tiny table at the side of the set. With network staff milling about, to her embarrassment, she dropped a spoon into her bowl of gazpacho. Red liquid sprayed her dress and his shirt.

He started laughing and told her, "Worst soup I've ever tasted, but it would work well in starting a food fight." He dipped his fingers in his bowl, reached across the table and smeared the cold tomato soup all over her face.

She took a dollop of sour cream and gently dropped it on his head. She burst out in laughter and felt like they were two silly kids having a good, messy time.

During much of her life, she allowed the darkness of fear to stop her from doing ordinary things. She thought, 'Test everything and hold onto what is good' (Thessalonians: 5:21). This was the time to discover what was good.

It was the time to learn to drive. Someday in the future, when Jared suggested an outing she could surprise him by picking him up at his place. Next time a man, hopefully Jared, asked her out on a date she'd happily accept. Next winter she'd make it a point to take ski lessons and learn to sail over snowy slopes.

By trying to please her parents, she had closed herself off from discovering new adventures and exploring God's majestic world.

She had allowed their fear of her dying to stop her from living.

Chapter Fifteen

XV
The Devil

In a quest to put her newfound confidence into practice, Cassandra accepted an invitation to attend a party. Given by one of the network's top executives, she wished Jared could return to New York and accompany her to the VIP's Sutton Place mansion.

Hours before the event, she started to feel a familiar, uncomfortable flurry of activity forming knots in her stomach. To distract her queasiness she immersed herself in research.

Unlike many people, including her parents, Cassandra didn't believe the devil existed as a separate entity. She believed evil emanated from and manifested itself within individuals.

Therefore, she felt intrigued rather than alarmed in researching the next Major Arcana labeled XV, The Devil. It, along with the Hangman and the Death cards, was at the center of why people associated tarot with the dark world of the occult.

The original Visconti-Sforza card was lost, but her deck included a card from another deck from the same timeframe. In addition, she studied other cards illustrated and released in different periods. Each told a similar symbolic story. The devil represented the Seven Capital Sins and the instigation of man's negative, base instincts.

The card served as a warning to practice Christian virtues in order to ward off the Devil and/or malevolence.

Without relying on Margo or Tomas, Cassandra prepared for the soirée. She chose a satin sheath, coordinating heels, and wore a freshwater pearl necklace. She applied makeup using only a hint of blush and pale peach lip-gloss. By now, she knew exactly how much oil to weave through her hair to prevent it from frizzing.

Sitting in the network's limo, a resurgence of nervousness began to fester. Fortunately, the ride was short.

At the party, among a group of strangers, she recognized a few familiar faces from the set. She smiled at them and everyone else.

One man rushed to her. "Thank you for the neat advice you gave me the other day. I now have a clearer picture of why my neighbor went ballistic. I've since apologized and have been respecting his boundaries."

"Glad to hear you restored peace."

"Have you considered becoming a life coach? Hearing some of the analogies you've given folks at work I think you have a rare ability to nail things in a hurry."

Surprised at his comment, she felt relieved when a waiter interrupted. Carrying a tray, he offered them champagne.

She took a piece of the delicate stemware and raised it to her lips.

Her coworker piped up, "Excuse me, Cassandra, while I get another beer."

While she milled around the crowd, Crystal bumped into her.

"Sorry. I've seemed to have lost my land legs."

With her free hand, Cassandra caught her wobbly body. "Want to go outside?"

"Sure. Lead the way."

Linking arms, they went out on the terrace.

"Guess I'm tipsy. Appreciate you rescuing me before I embarrassed myself."

"Want some water?"

She nodded.

Cassandra exchanged her champagne flute for two tumblers filled with ice water. She handed one to Crystal. "I don't think I've thanked you for your gracious acceptance on my first day at the network."

"I must admit I felt a little sorry for you." A hiccup caused her body to jump.

"I certainly must have been a sight."

"No, no. You looked fine and you look wonderful right now." She took a long drink of water. "You seemed like such a sweet naïve kid. I was concerned you'd be swallowed up by our corrupt world."

"I don't understand."

"For one thing, I thought Jared would add you to his list of conquests and shatter your innocence. Noticed he's not with you. Good for you, girl, I can see you know how to handle yourself with or without him. Has he moved onto his next project?" With one hand, she covered her mouth. With the other, she shoved the water glass at Cassandra before dashing away.

Maybe Jared was a womanizer, but he had always treated Cassandra with respect. Apparently, he wasn't interested in seducing her. She felt pleased he hadn't taken advantage of her wild attraction toward him, but concurrently she felt slighted by him treating her like a friend rather than a desirable female.

When she heard about his reputation with women, she secretly felt jealous of the lovely ladies who had aroused his manly interest. She wished he desired her in a way he had never desired anyone else. She wanted to be his forever woman, his permanent love. She deluded herself in believing she could change him from a playboy into the marrying type of guy she yearned for in her heart.

Crystal's remarks reminded Cassandra of innuendos made by other coworkers. Until that moment, she discounted insinuations of her being romantically involved with Jared. In general, she felt flattered by such comments. It boosted her esteem to have her associates believe she was his sweetheart. Rather than considering the rumors a blemish on her reputation, she felt pleased to have others think this famous personality had chosen to shower his affection on her.

A middle-aged man tapped her on the shoulder. "Are you there?"

His touch brought her back to the party. "Sorry."

"Hi. I'm Ethan. I narrate the History Hour."

"I'm…"

"I know. You're the lovely Cassandra. I understand you're researching tarot cards. Must be interesting. Which one are you working on?"

Glad he mentioned a topic within her comfort zone she easily replied, "The sixteenth Major Arcana, XV, The Devil."

His eyes widened, his lips curled, and he wiggled his fingers. "Woo-hoo. Tell me about the prince of darkness tempting us by fame, fortune, and carnal pleasures."

"When the devil or temptations, stand between a person and God, only darkness is visible."

"Is darkness meant to be feared? Is it as strong as light?"

"No. Light is energy and God, the true light, is all-powerful. Darkness isn't the opposite of light. It's merely the absence of light. Therefore, darkness doesn't have power on its own. While the devil can act as a shadow dimming the light and temptation can weaken our ability to view the light, we have the capability and choice to either remove the shadow or not."

"Are you saying we're stronger than the devil?"

"The devil doesn't have the power to make us act. He can only entice us, lure our souls into dark places. At those times, a person may choose to worship the creation instead of the Creator. But remember, every person has the power to overcome temptations in order to see the light and the truth."

She didn't want to monopolize the conversation, "What about you? What are you working on?"

"The hidden secrets of the Kalahari Desert."

"Tell me more."

He rambled off statistics before saying, "I'd love you to join my team. Bet I can double whatever Jared's paying you. And believe me, unlike him, I can make you famous."

Although she wasn't prepared to take his offer she felt a tinge of temptation. It would be exciting to gain status in show business and the lure of a sizable income could satisfy her new acquired taste for finer things in life especially being able to afford traveling.

He told her, "I'd really like to spend more time with you, socially. Want to go to dinner?"

Although she enjoyed their discussion, she wasn't tempted to date him. Besides, she was too infatuated with Jared to be interested in any other man.

Thinking of what to say, she hesitated.

He took her hands in his. He lowered his head. With a rough push, he placed his opened mouth over her lips.

When she didn't respond to his kiss, Ethan said, "Or can I tempt you into coming up to my apartment?" He winked, "If you're ready to end your romp with Jared, I'll be happy to take his place."

She pulled herself free. "Tonight I'm not tempted by darkness." She turned and briskly walked away.

On the ride back to her hotel, the ramifications and dangers of the gossip she and Jared generated dawned on her. People weren't thinking she and Jared were friends or innocently flirting. They concluded she and Jared were having a sordid affair.

Since she began working with Jared, how many times had she been tempted to abandon her parents' moral blueprint? How many times had she wanted to throw herself into his arms? How many times had she envied the women he had lusted after?

A deep shame poured like rain from her head to her heart. She had allowed glamorous temptations of the rich, famous, and handsome Jared to overshadow her core values.

She wished she could step out of herself, stand at her side, and see herself more clearly. She wondered.

Was she so lonely for attention she ignored the real Jared?

Was she so tired of being criticized she believed his false flattery?

Was she so hungry for affection she believed he was falling in love with her?

Thoughts of tarot filled her mind. In particular, she envisioned the many depictions of the Devil card. In each card, the Lovers, Adam and Eve could voluntarily remove the chains loosely encircling their necks.

Cassandra had the same ability. She could remove the chains of illusion before they weighed her down into the depths of complete darkness. By accepting reality, she could eradicate the mantel of desire enslaving her heart.

It was time to recognize the truth, and stop lusting after a man who didn't desire her. She had to end the immature crush she felt for her boss and accept the limits of their professional relationship. Truth was she mistook his respectful treatment, his friendship, as a sign he would fall in love with her. Basing her hope on fiction rather than truth, she felt tempted by unrealistic images of a future with Jared.

When being kind to Jared, to become his true friend, she needed to stop having an ulterior motive. Rather than trying to tempt him into falling in love with her, she needed to embrace tarot's symbolism referring to the Bible teaching us the conduit to God is through service to others.

Despite having heard parts of the Holy Scriptures at school and during Masses, until she researched tarot, Cassandra hadn't studied the Bible. As she gained a deeper understanding of sacred teachings, she simultaneously felt strengthened by the profound reassurance they offered.

In the next instant, another haunting tarot message stirred her thoughts. The Devil card was the blame card.

Guilty feelings for holding her parents responsible for her estrangement from them dampened her mood.

It was time for her to address the anger she felt toward them. It was time to stop blaming them. It was time to forgive them. It was time to recognize the pain she caused them by straying from their nest.

Desperately wanting to heal, repair, and strengthen her damaged relationship with her parents, Cassandra hoped she had the ability to accept how they felt about her.

Chapter Sixteen

XVI
The Tower

On the following Saturday morning, Cassandra phoned her mother. When her call went to voicemail, she left a message, "I'm sorry to have hurt you. I'll be arriving in New Haven at eleven so we can talk in person. I love you."

She quickly dressed and took a cab to Grand Central Station.

En route to Connecticut, she studied the seventeenth Major Arcana labeled XVI, The Tower. Like the Devil card because the original was lost the deck contained a replacement card from the same period.

She recalled reading during the Renaissance the card had several names including Thunderbolt, Fire, House of the Damned, House of Pluto or Hell. Negative interpretations focused on biblical punishments of the prideful builders of the tower of Babel and of Heaven using fire and brimstone to destroy Sodom and Gomorrah.

At New Haven Station, Cassandra felt disappointed. She hadn't received a call from her mother and no one was waiting for her on the platform. She took a cab to her parents' house. Although there weren't any cars in the driveway, it didn't mean they weren't home. They often pulled their vehicles into the garage to protect them from sunny or rainy weather.

She slowly walked up to the door trying to decide if she should use her key.

Under the strained circumstances, she decided to ring the bell.

After several minutes, her mother opened the door.

Cassandra embraced her, "Hi Mom."

Her mother's arms remained at her sides. She didn't return her daughter's greeting.

Cassandra followed her mother into the sunroom where her father was sitting and sat across from him.

Without rising, he spoke in his usual monotone voice. "Well young lady, what do you have to say for yourself?"

"I'm sorry to have displeased you, but I'd like to explain…"

"The only thing that will make this right is you quitting your foolish tarot research."

She closed her eyes for a moment and prayed for patience.

She asked, "Have you had a chance to speak to Father Jorge?"

"When was the last time you went to Mass? Maybe if you were practicing your faith you'd know evil when you saw it."

"Aren't you sorry for what you did to my apartment?"

"All I did was pay some men to help you see God's light, but you're too influenced by the devil incarnate, that Jared fellow. Because of him you're blind and can't see goodness."

She couldn't believe her father was so prejudice, so self righteous, so arrogant. Hadn't he learned anything from being arrested? "Dad, what you did was illegal."

"In expressing obedience to a higher law, I would have gladly gone to jail."

"Tell me what law you were obeying?"

Her mother answered, "Child, if you can't even recognize God's law you're too far gone for us to explain anything to you. Why don't you visit Father Jorge? Maybe he's have the right words to explain the truth."

Cassandra made an effort to speak softly. "You're my parents and whether we understand each other or not, I'll always love you. I don't mean to hurt you."

"Then why won't you quit Jared's show?"

"Mom, Dad, I don't advocate using tarot cards to predict the future. For that matter, I don't defend their use at all. I'm just researching them. In doing so, I can't help but notice they provide a path to God."

Her mother shouted, "That path you speak of can lead to false gods. Can you deny the occult uses tarot?"

"No. But one fact doesn't tell the entire truth."

"That one fact is enough for me. Why isn't it for you? "

"Unless all facts are known one isolated fact can be misleading?"

"Child I'm not alone in denouncing tarot. Most God fearing people see their danger. Most good people avoid them."

"I'm not denying if misused tarot can be dangerous. I'm only reporting their original intentions."

"Millions of people can't be wrong."

"Millions of people followed Hitler while only twelve followed Christ."

Her father stood and moved closer to her. It was one of the few times she'd seen him show emotion. His face was red with rage. "How dare you speak to your mother that way?"

Her mother held up her hand and glanced at him. "It's okay, dear. Once Cassie is cleansed she's see the truth." She turned to Cassandra. "Trust me. The truth is tarot cards, all of them, are evil."

"Mom can't you see the difference between brainwashing and cleansing?"

Her father said, "We have nothing more to say. Don't come back here until you've seen the light."

She thought, *Fear and intimidation aren't the light. In His gentleness, loving Christ is the light and the truth.*

Heartbroken, she left their house. She called a cab to pick her up. While she waited, she thought her parents would mellow to the point of welcoming her back inside, but they didn't.

At the train station, she sat on a hard wooden bench and tried to accept her parents' position.

Her cell rang. Hoping it was her mother or father, without looking at the caller ID, she cheerfully answered, "Glad you called."

"Thank you," Jared responded. "I just got back in town. Have any free time today?"

She suggested they meet for dinner.

By the time she entered her hotel suite, it was late afternoon.

She slipped in the shower, and as she rinsed her hair, she wished she could wash away her sadness.

Just before leaving to meet Jared, she stared out the window and looked down into Central Park. She saw a young child holding her mother and father's hands. Every so often, the parents lifted their little girl in the air. Although Cassandra couldn't see the girl's face she imaged the child laughing. She remembered times her parents played the same game and delighted her. Tears welled in her eyes. She hoped they also cherished many joyous memories.

She glanced at her watch realizing she should have left minutes earlier. Dashing toward her destination, she contained her unhappiness by focusing on being a supportive friend for Jared.

As soon as she walked through the doors of the casual restaurant, Cassandra spotted him sitting in a booth.

As she got closer, dark circles under his eyes reflected his inner pain.

"Hi, there." She patted his shoulder. "How you doing?" She sat across from him.

"My visit refreshed the reality of why I don't visit my father. So caught up in spouting chapter and verse, he didn't let down his defenses. I don't know why I expected things to be different. All through my growing years, he used the Bible as a wall between us. Maybe it's his pride. Even though we're the only family each of have, he continued to stay at a distance from me."

"I'm sorry."

"No big deal. Like I said, I was foolish to expect anything else from him." He laughed. "Maybe I deserve my dad's indifference. I get his point. I'm the one who left."

"But you went to him during his time of grief."

"I went for my sake not his. He has his faith to help him accept Sue's death. What do I have?"

"You have your work."

"It feels like everything's crumbling around me. I'm almost certain the network won't renew my contract and rightfully so. I'm getting stale." In the next breath, he asked," How about you? Have you seen your folks?"

"I went to visit them earlier today, but having fallen from their graces, they banished me from what they consider their pious home. I'll admit I feel unsteady, miserable, and quite sad. It's as though I've lost my equilibrium. I'm questioning my ideologies and beliefs. It's as though my former persona is gone forever. My personality, my appearance, my job, my entire life seems shaky. All I'm sure of is I can't go back to working in a tiny office cubicle."

He chuckled and took her hands in his. "It seems we're both in limbo. So much of what we believed were certainties are collapsing."

She sighed. "In my case, maybe the past needs to crumble in order for me to rebuild a better future. With my old images shattered, it's up to me to pick up the broken pieces and clean up the mess I helped create."

"What did you do?"

"I blindly followed my parents' script. I didn't question their authority. I didn't make my own judgments. Since I realized my part in this ugly drama, I tried to tell them I'm sorry for hurting them.

"Right now, they're not ready to hear what I have to say. While they think things over, I'm going to try to use the time to discern between who they think I should be and who I am."

Chapter Seventeen

XVII
The Star

After dinner, Jared's driver drove them from Manhattan to Brooklyn. He pulled the limo into a parking lot.

Not familiar with the area Cassandra asked, "Where are we?"

"Near the pedestrian entrance of the Brooklyn Bridge." Jared asked, "Have you ever walked across this iconic landmark?"

"No, I haven't, but after such a big meal I think it might be a good idea to take a stroll. And I'm glad I have my Italian coat to keep me warm."

Above auto lanes, they leisurely trailed behind a tour group onto the walkway located in the center of the bridge. "Do you know much about the structure?"

"Only that I've admired its architecture."

"Finally I can tell an historian a bit of history."

She giggled.

He proudly explained, "With the help of six hundred workers it took fourteen years to build. As the longest cable-stayed/suspension bridge of its day it opened in 1883 and is currently one of oldest bridges of its type in America."

For no apparent reason, Jared wrapped his arms around Cassandra and in one smooth motion lifted her off the ground. His lips briefly brushed hers before he twirled around causing her red coat to flare and swing.

In the next moment, he put her feet back on the ground, uncoiled his arms, and reached for her hand.

On this moonless night, with stars dancing in the dark sky, his tender touch ignited a longing within her.

Although it was the first time he had crossed the line from acting like a friend to being somewhat romantic, she reminded herself not to read too much into his innocent behavior. She assumed in his state of mourning he was simply seeking solace.

Yet, she couldn't calm her stirring passion.

As they continued, she noticed couples nuzzling their heads together. A few stole a kiss or two.

To divert her attention from the lovers, she peered beyond the bridge to the East River. With her free hand, she pointed to the shimmering surface. "It's as if we're floating over painted glass.

He didn't comment.

Her gaze turned forward. "Having only seen the towers from a distance I never realized how large they are. And their sculptured lines made them exceedingly attractive."

"They're made of limestone, granite, and Rosendale cement. A little known fact is to help fund the bridge's construction cost, the city rented vaults under the bridge before its completion. Merchants stored wine in the constant sixty-degree vaults. They're called the Blue Grotto because a shrine to the Virgin Mary was next to its entrance.

With our country's Judeo-Christian roots, she wondered how many other places in the city reflected religious significance.

Jared continued, "The entire engineering feat stood as a symbol of optimism to the people of this great town."

After passing under the towers, Cassandra stared at New York City's skyline.

Jared said, "From this angle the view is magnificent, a true testimony to man's creativity."

"Creativity inspired by God. Humans, like the stars are God's creations. Both can shine."

"Or extinguish like Sue."

Cassandra silently shared Jared's sorrow.

He broke the stillness by saying, "I'm trying to keep her sense of hope shinning in my heart, but it's hard."

She squeezed his fingertips. "Wish I had gotten to know her better."

"Too bad you didn't see her at her best. She had a great sense of humor. Even at the worst times when I was hurting real bad, she'd make me smile." He pulled his hand free from hers and cupped his ear. As if listening to a distant memory he paused. "I can almost hear her infectious laugh. And when she was serious, she had the power to encourage me to dream, dream big. If it hadn't been for her I wouldn't have become a TV star. Too bad fame blinded me from seeing what really matters."

"Which is?"

"Helping people."

"Isn't it beneficial to stimulate people to think?"

"Maybe, but I haven't improved the lives of those I care about most." Without giving her a chance to ask questions, he changed the subject from personal to business. "I assume the tarot ghost is still haunting you. What card are you working on?"

Guessing he wanted to take a detour from his overwhelming emotions, she rattled off a summary. "The eighteenth tarot card is labeled XVII, The Star. The Visconti-Sforza deck depicts a young blonde woman wearing a light blue dress embroidered with gold. A red cloak decorated with golden stars rests on her shoulders. She's holding an eight pointed star in her left hand."

"What does it mean?"

"In the Zodiac Venus represents the Virgin Mary, figure of peace, goodness, and serenity. She's the mother of God and stands for hope."

"Venus is a planet."

"True. Along with the sun and moon, it's part of the luminous triad. Shinning at dawn, Venus is known as the morning star."

"I remember Christ referring to himself as the morning star. 'I Jesus have sent my angel to give you this testimony for the churches. I am the root and offspring of David and the bright morning star' (Revelation: 22:11)."

"Indeed. Jesus Christ is the light of the world. According to some interpretations, He's the star of tarot. And the twenty-two Major Arcana, form a pathway to His light."

"Now that my mind is recalling my father's biblical references, I have a vague recollection of Satan also being called the morning star. Know anything about that?"

"When referring to Satan's fall from Heaven, Isaiah refers to him as the morning star. Remember Satan was created and isn't self-existent like Christ is. Thus, Satan is only a poor imitation of the true morning star."

"Of course. Now I remember my dad referring to Satan as an imposter. What else does the card symbolize?"

"Other interpretations refer to Dante's intellectual and spiritual journey. After leaving hell, casting his eyes on the stars renewed his sense of hope.

"In short, tarot's Star card symbolizes Jesus and his goodness. It embodies enlightened ideas, beauty, art, and above all the love that guides living beings. The card reflects harmony between people."

"Is that its practical message?"

"It, also, offers an invitation for each of us to be introspective. It suggests we identify and examine our inner contradictions. It recommends we seek to discover personal lessons attached to the trials of existence we face." Realizing she was bordering on being esoteric, she asked, "What do the stars mean to you?"

He stood at her side and gazed upward. "Whew. Being with my dad must really have made an impact on my unconscious. The moment I looked at the sky Psalm 19:1 popped into my mind. 'The Heavens declare the glory of God; the skies proclaim the works of his hands'."

"Once again, the Bible reminds us to worship the Creator not His creations."

"And you? What do you see?"

Feeling a special connection between them, Cassandra shared, "The sky filled with stars reminds me of the countless sparkling moments I've experienced since I met you."

Chapter Eighteen

XVIII
The Moon

Working closely with the scriptwriters, Cassandra felt astounded by their talents. They turned her raw, sometimes boring data into compelling, interesting commentaries. It was as if they were creating a tarot tapestry, vivid, colorful, and rich with detail. They pulled threads of ideas from the card's beginning images into each subsequent one to create explanatory word pictures.

Sitting in a room filled with upholstered chairs and sofas, the mood felt relaxed. In the casual atmosphere, she had no trouble exchanging ideas.

From her notes and comments regarding the tarot deck's nineteenth Major Arcana, labeled XVIII, The Moon, the group spent hours brainstorming.

Included in their packets, in order for them to see the details more clearly, she had included enlarged photos of the Visconti-Sforza card. The Moon card depicted a woman with thigh length blonde hair. A lilac tunic, decorated with a string of golden crosses at the scoop neckline, covered much of her light blue dress. In her right hand, she held a crescent moon. In her left, she clutched reins.

Cassandra ended their session by saying. "I think you've captured the essence of the card. I especially like your conclusion stating, 'Besides reining in the oceans by controlling their tides, the moon influences natural rhythms even within humans.'"

As the group members filed out of the room, Bev, the script director still sitting on an oversized armchair asked Cassandra, "Got a sec?"

"Sure. Have questions about the upcoming schedule?"

"More specifically, I was wondering what you plan to do after you finish the tarot segment?"

"I'm not sure. In a broad sense, I'd like to focus on historical research which can reveal little known truths."

"With your tenacity, I'm sure you'll be a success in whatever you pursue." She cleared her throat. "I want to congratulate you. Just as I predicted, you didn't let Jared win our little bet?"

"What bet?" From the glint in Bev's eyes, Cassandra was sorry she asked.

"Hasn't he told you?"

Not sure if she wanted to hear what Bev had to say, Cassandra shrugged her shoulders.

"Guess I'll just have to enlighten you." She crossed her legs and clasped her hands in her lap. "Some time ago, he professed his belief that anyone was corruptible. My opinion, similar to the cliché, you can't cheat an honest man, was some people's Christian faith is unbreakable. Jared's view, in short, was there are neither honest men nor any people of unshakable faith."

As if bracing herself for a blow, Cassandra felt all her weight lean on her heels and her fingers tightly grip her notepad.

Bev moved her torso forward. "Jared came up with the hypothesis of television's glitz and glamour being powerful enough to change anyone. To prove his point, he set out to find just the right subject for his experiment.

"He chose you because you epitomized a sheltered Catholic girl. As an historian, despite your lack of life experience, he was certain it would be an easy enough task for you to research tarot.

"He conjectured, in a short amount of time you'd become like any of us pros, selfish and greedy. Tempted by the fast lane you'd abandon your faith, or at least put it on hold, and indulge in the sorted world of show biz."

Bev's words like a poison dart burst Cassandra's illusion of Jared. Its venom raced through her blood stream spreading a sickening sensation to every part of her body. She simultaneously ached, felt dizzy, had the chills, and was sick to her stomach.

Bev's voice droned on, "He was elated by your Visconti name. It was the deciding factor in him choosing you over other contenders."

Cassandra's head throbbed with intense emotional pain. She realized she denied what was obvious to everyone around her. Now Crystal and other people's remarks about her being one of Jared's projects made sense.

Bev glanced at her watch and stood up. "Got to run." In the next second, she walked out of the room leaving Cassandra alone with her distressing thoughts.

Her body slid down into the soft armchair. With her eyes closed, she wondered. *Was she like the moon, a dead entity, lacking her own energy source? Like the moon reflecting the sun's light, was she only capable of reflecting someone else's ideas?*

Until she met Jared, she reflected her parents' opinions, points of views, attitudes, morals, and religious beliefs. Since she worked with him, she reflected Jared's zeal to produce positive aspects of tarot.

Ironically, in the guise of searching for truth, she denied the reality of substituting one controlling figure in her life for another.

But Cassandra had changed. As she thought of her reinvented self, a serene calmness liberated her from discomforting feelings.

A vivid clarity bolstered her spirits.

She was no longer the naïve girl Jared had handpicked for his experiment. She was an adult woman who unveiled inner strengths and convictions. Having gained confidence, she freely shared analogies attempting to help others problem-solve.

 In the process of researching tarot, she had grown to a higher spiritual level.

Bev's revelation didn't matter. Cassandra's evolution stood as a testimony refuting Jared's theory.

Despite his devastating betrayal, she had control of her life. To exercise her power, she had to end her enmeshment with Jared.

Before going back to the Plaza, Cassandra went shopping. She instructed her driver to wait while she visited various shops. She kept returning to the car handing him her many purchases.

He told her, "I can wait by each store. You can have your packages sent out to me."

"No thank you." She didn't want to take his advice or anyone else's.

She tried on clothes she liked. Not caring what her mother or Margo would think, she purchased outfits she deemed pleasing.

By the time she had ended her shopping spree, the sun had already set.

The driver said, "Take a gander at the full moon. Glad I can go straight home, 'cause I'd hate to be on the road with a town full of lunatics."

Although she didn't reply, she felt she, too, might be mad.

Up in her hotel room she stripped out of her clothes and placed them in a dry cleaning bag. She slipped into a new pair of pajamas. She looked around the suite. Nothing belonged to her, nor would she miss anything from the luxurious surroundings. The one exception was the coat Jared had bought her in Milan.

She longed to have a place of her own filled with objects of her choosing and taste. Since the ransacking and restoration of her apartment, knowing she could never live there again, she had paid off the remainder of her lease. Therefore, she needed to search for another place to live.

Early next morning, she contacted a realtor. After learning about the limited inventory of rentals, she snatched up a new listing. It was a tiny one bedroom flat, convenient to the subway, but farther from her job. Although it was more expensive than her previous apartment, she thought, with the money she earned from the tarot assignment, she'd be able to afford it.

Surfing her computer, she spent a few hours shopping online to purchase essentials. Wanting to buy just the right pieces to complement her new space, she decided to take her time decorating.

While she packed her clothes in luggage she had purchased, the Moon tarot card haunted her. Like the moon, Jared was a pretender, a liar. He wasn't what he appeared to be. He seemed humble. Yet, all the while, he deceived her. He wasn't a man of honor. He was an egotist who believed he knew all there was to know about human nature in general and her personality in particular.

She gathered her research notes and computer. She stacked them in a box.

Although she didn't think she'd be able to wear her red, swing coat again, she decided not to leave it at the hotel. Sometime in the future, she'd donate it to a women's shelter. With it draped over her arm, she took a taxi to her empty apartment. With the help of the cabdriver, she placed the suitcases in her bedroom and the box in the living room.

While she hung a new coat in the entryway closet, with a pang of sadness, not wanting a reminder of Jared, she folded her red coat and shoved it to the back of the closet's highest shelf. She checked with the building's superintendent to be certain he would accept delivery of the mattress and bed linens she had ordered.

Setting out to shop for groceries, she passed a Catholic Church. A block later, she decided to turn around and retrace her steps.

Not sure if the church was open at this time of day, she nevertheless tried the main door. It easily swung into a vestibule. As if welcoming her inside, a set of French doors were pinned back in an opened position. She walked down the wide aisle. The expansive space was hushed. A few people were kneeling and praying.

While taking a seat in a pew, a familiar reassure enveloped her. Rather than feeling alone on a barren sphere, she felt connected to God.

Noticing people entering and exiting a confessional, to quell her pangs of guilt, without hesitation, she filed in line. When it was her turn, she told the priest about her tarot assignment and her parents' estrangement. "I take full responsibility for wounding them. But wish they would forgive me."

He advised, "Give them time my child."

She tried to explain her attraction to the temptations of wealth and glamour. "Father I'm confused and uncertain if I'm following God's path."

"Why do you doubt your decisions?"

"Because I'm not sure I've been true to myself, my values, or my faith."

He patiently waited while she elaborated. "I was so intent on searching for the truth about tarot I didn't notice I was surrounded by lies. Tempted to be close to someone famous, I fell in love with a dishonorable man."

She felt deep shame. "By being egotistical, I've greatly sinned"

"Who have you hurt by doing your job? Who will be hurt by you providing the history of tarot on television?

Who will suffer from you having loving feelings toward your boss?"

Cassandra was silent. She tried to think of how her research could hurt anyone, how her infatuation for Jared could hurt others. "I'm the only one who could be hurt."

"How so?"

"I may never regain my parents' respect. And because of shattered romantic dreams, I'm the one who will continue to suffer."

"Oh, I see. Then it's about you? Without your parents' approval and your boss's love your ego remains bruised. In short, it's about your pain, your loss, your disillusionment."

His words stunned her. Yet, she knew he was right. Feeling grateful, she thanked the priest for his insights.

His kindness came through his voice as he gave her absolution. He listed prayers for her to recite. "As part of your penance I recommend you complete your assignment without thinking of what people will think of you. Focus on historical facts and share them with your audience. Give folks the dignity to make up their own minds. I repeat. Tell the truth regardless of what others think of you."

She understood his reasoning. She had made a commitment to her supervisor, to Jared, and to herself. She had to honor her contract. She had to do her job to the best of her ability without worrying about the opinions of others.

She exited the confessional, slipped into a pew and knelt on her knees. While saying her prayers of penance, a joy filled her heart. She felt a rejuvenation of God's light within her.

When she stood, she felt God's light shining within her. Like an epiphany, she felt a simple, yet profound enlightening message resounding in her mind. *Rather than redefining herself, she could benefit others most from just being herself, Cassandra Angelica Visconti, a child of God.*

Chapter Nineteen

XIX
The Sun

Without curtains, dawn's first light filtered through her bedroom window and pierced the darkness. Its soft glow awakened Cassandra. She stretched her arms over her head and felt a myriad of emotions. Regardless of her good feelings, she couldn't shake a deep sorrow weighing heavily on her heart. She couldn't rid her mind of conflicting thoughts.

Over the last few days, although Jared had phoned and left several text messages, she opted not to respond. Characterizing his behaviors as betrayal, she understood why her parents chose not to speak to her. Like them, in order to heal, she needed time to accept reality.

She peered out the window and watched the sunrise. A festive, soft pink banner accented with muted reds hovered over the horizon. As the bright star rose higher, layers of luminescence appeared in a powder blue sky. She felt an inner stirring. It was as if God's light was nudging her to move forward.

She realized her first step on her continuing journey was to forgive Jared, but worried she'd once again succumb to his charms. She felt anxious about her involuntary carnal passions tempting her to the point of distorting her sense of reason.

Before seeing him, she decided to clarify her thoughts. Without a doubt, his experiment was a repulsive, despicable trick.

Yet, despite his motivations, in choosing her as his subject, he gave Cassandra opportunities to grow. She couldn't deny her appreciation for all he had shown her and all he had given her.

She simultaneously hated him and loved him.

As she stared at the ball of fire ushering in the day, she thought of its capabilities. The sun, our main source of warmth can also burn us. Its light can sweep away shadows and allow us to see clearly, but too much light can blind us.

Jared, like the sun, had the ability to affect her in positive and negative ways.

Part of her wanted to confront him, but another part wanted to protect her self-esteem from further humiliation. She vowed, once she completed her assignment, her association with him would end. Because he concurrently meant nothing and everything to her, she'd have to garner all her strength to fulfill her self-promise.

From her mattress resting directly on the floor, she scooted over to her makeshift cardboard box desk in the adjoining room. While her computer warmed up, she studied the twentieth Visconti-Sforza tarot card labeled, XIX, The Sun. It depicted a naked, winged angel standing on a cloud suspended in the sky. A long scarf rested on his shoulders and a coral necklace encircled his neck. He held a face radiating light. It represented intelligence and rationality.

Spiritually, the tarot card emphasized the sun is the highest physical symbol of God. More specifically, the sun represents the son of God, Jesus Christ. The sun gives earthly life. Jesus gives eternal life. The sun is the source of illumination, warmth, and survival. Christ is the source of truth, comfort, and never ending existence.

The Book of Revelation describes the sun perpetually shinning. Science confirms, even when the earth blocks the sun's light and causes night to envelop us, the sun constantly radiates its light. Likewise, the Bible tells us God is always there for us even when the shadows of temptation block Him from our view.

Unlike the duality of the sun, the Son of God is everlastingly good. Moreover, God always offers a union between Himself, the Creator, and us, his creation.

Wealth, whether material, intellectual, or spiritual are associated with the sun. Each of these states holds its own value. Some are more precious than gold. For example, by using logic we can achieve clarity of self and others.

The tarot card implied transparency was necessary to create true harmony, friendship, love, and happiness.

She attempted to apply tarot's messages to her situation. Rational thought could shed light on the superficial facts Bev had provided. Rather than overreacting to part of the story, Cassandra's future depended upon lucidity.

Until she saw Jared, she wouldn't be able to separate the tangled threads of ambiguity from those of certainty.

She texted him and asked if they could meet.

Five minutes later he called, "Hi. Is anything wrong? I feel as if you've been avoiding me."

She disregarded his question. "I'll be at the studio later today. Do you have a few minutes to see me?"

"Of course, stop by my office anytime."

After meeting with the scriptwriters, she knocked on Jared's office door.

He responded, "Come in."

As she stepped into his professional space, he pushed his chair back, rose, and walked toward her.

Before she could stop him, he wrapped his arms around her. "I have a confession to make. I started our relationship under false pretenses."

Not wanting her physical desire to influence her decision, she wriggled out of his embrace. "Bev told me about the bet you two made."

His penetrating dark eyes stared into hers. "I wanted to change you by creating you into the image I held in my mind of a glamorous pagan. But the real you kept shining through. Sure, I laid it on thick upping your salary, splurging on the expensive Plaza suite, buying you designer clothes, and taking you to Italy, but no matter how hard I tried to entice you, I couldn't sway you from your core beliefs. I couldn't dissuade you from seeking God's path."

Hearing him admit the truth felt like a hammer slamming her already crushed heart. To avoid sinking into a depressed state, she had to respond rationally.

She took a long breath before outlining her plan. "I came here today to tell you three things.

"First, I forgive you.

"Second, I'll complete my contract and finish my research for the tarot segment.

"Third, after our work is completed I never want to see you again." She turned to leave.

He reached for her arm and held it. "Always the seeker of truth, you constantly reveal the basic elements of your personality. You value your dreams no matter how idealistic. You believe in drawing upon inner knowledge. You're honest and authentic in everything you do. You constantly repeat a pattern of seeking God's path."

Thinking his compliments empty and merely spoken to confuse her, she told him. "In light of your actions, your words are meaningless."

"Beyond a doubt, I'm the devil who tried to tempt you, corrupt you, but you seduced me. You seduced me into Christianity. A faith my father tried to pound into me, and one I fervently resisted."

He took hold of her other arm and gently turned her directly toward him. "After seeing the affect you had on Sue, I could no longer deny your role in my conversion. Because of you I believe in the Lord."

She swallowed a lump of skepticism.

He released her arms. "In all my planning, what I never expected was I would be the one to change. Moreover, I never expected to fall in love with you. Your glowing spirit, your beauty, and your magnificent truth overcame my deceit, overpowered my resolve, and overwhelmed me with heated passion. Even though I've lost you, I'm grateful for what the experiment did for me. It gave me faith and filled me with love."

He lowered his gaze. "But there I go again only thinking of myself, wishing you'd give me one more chance, wishing you'd give me hope."

She felt a longing to caress him, but she resisted.

Raising his stare, Jared kept explaining, "I'm sorry I injured you. It was never my intent to hurt you. I thought it only natural for you or anyone to surrender to the temptations of the so-called good life.

"But you shamed me. You showed me, through your living example, the true riches in our world."

He lowered his head and kissed the top of hers. "Thank you for all you've given me."

Trying to deny her love for him, she dismissed him by saying, "Your dramatic words rather than sounding sincere reek of showmanship. Instead of wasting your eloquence on me, you'd be more successful, if you showered your talents on the *Fact or Truth* tarot segment."

Without expecting or waiting for a response, she left his office.

Chapter Twenty

XX
Judgment

As Cassandra rushed out of the building, stormy clouds rolled across the sky. By the time she exited the subway station, rain pounded the streets. While running home, without the aid of an umbrella, she was quickly drenched. The weather conditions were reminiscent of the day she first reported to the studio to begin her tarot assignment.

During the months since then, it seemed as if her life had recreated itself several times.

Once inside her apartment, she changed into dry clothes, wrapped a blanket around her shoulders, and sipped hot tea from a paper cup. Regardless, of her attempts to keep warm she couldn't shake an invasive dampness. A dull gloominess descended upon the empty space surrounding her and pressed upon a barren space within her.

Thoughts of Jared's experiment filled her mind and troubled her heart. As if entombed by the constraints of her limiting situation, a lack of hope left her feeling something inside her had died.

Involuntarily, she wept for Jared's tragic loss. Sue was a woman she hardly knew, but greatly missed. Death had the power, with or without warning, to snatch away a loved one. It was no wonder many people feared it and cloaked it in mysterious darkness.

Cassandra shuddered, but couldn't dispel her morbid thoughts. She felt tempted to crawl on her mattress, bury herself under the covers, and cry. To stop her self-pitying, she forced herself to continue researching tarot.

The sooner she completed the task, the faster she could distance herself from the man she loved.

Sitting in front of her makeshift desk, she studied the Visconti-Sforza tarot deck's twenty-first Major Arcana labeled XX, Judgment. At the bottom of the card, a young man and young woman sitting in a casket were praying. Between them, a bearded man's face looked upward. At the top of the card, God the Father wearing a crown held a sword in His right hand and a globe in His left. Two angels playing trumpets were at His sides.

The angels reminded her of biblical references to judgment day. In particular, she thought, 'And he will send out his angels with a trumpet blast, and they will gather his elect from the four winds, from one end of the heavens to the other' (Mathew 24:31). '… tombs were opened, and the bodies of many saints who had fallen asleep were raised' (Mathew 27: 52).

The message of this card was clear. One day each of us, young or old, would face our Creator and His judgment. She thought of God's warning. 'Stop judging, that you may not be judged' (Mathew 7:1).

In her arrogance, had she talked down to her parents? Had she labeled them narrow minded? Why had she been more concerned with them rejecting her, than her attempting to understand them? Rather than judging them, she could focus on their good intentions. She could accept their love albeit at a distance.

The ring of her cell interrupted her thoughts. When she read the ID screen she quickly answered, "Hi Mom."

"Cassandra, we love you and always will."

"Me too. I'm sorry if… "

Her mother talked over Cassandra's words, "We met with Father Jorge. He helped us see it's God job, not ours to judge. He helped us see you haven't done anything wrong. Please forgive us for mistrusting you."

The two women warmly chatted for almost an hour. Her mother ended the call by saying, "We have no ill feelings toward Jared, either. If he makes you happy, we'd welcome him in our home, your home."

Having her parents back in her life offered Cassandra great relief. Unaware of Jared's deception, it was easy for her mother not to judge him. Yet, her mother's statement led to Cassandra questioning herself.

Had she judged Jared?

Had she condemned him?

Why was she so quick to dismiss his apology?

Why did she rush to banish him from her life?

She thought of the ultimate judgment day following her death. What she and most people wanted was for God to show mercy.

Hadn't she forgiven Jared?

Wasn't that enough?

What more could she do?

What more did she want from God?

The answer was unmistakable. She wanted God to give her a second, third chance, no an infinite number of chances to do what was right.

Why wasn't she willing to put Jared's transgression into perspective? He was a good man. He wasn't an abusive person who would intentionally injure her again and again until he killed her spirit.

Why couldn't she view his behavior as a misguided event?

Regardless of his motivations or intentions, through his experiment, she found more joy than she ever dreamed possible.

Then why couldn't she show him mercy?

Then why was she refusing to shower him with love?

She unconsciously flipped through the tarot deck.

The Lovers card came into view.

The answer although symbolic appeared as bold as if it written in red ink, EGO.

Chapter Twenty-One

XXI
The World

Following the national debut of *Fact or Truth's* tarot segment, Cassandra stared at the Visconti-Sforza deck's Major Arcana labeled XXI, The World. It depicted two angels with small blue wings. Clothed only in thin red scarves, their hands reached up. They held a picture of a castle sitting on an island under a sky dusted with stars.

The image referred to *Civitas dei*, the Celestial Jerusalem described in The Revelation of St. John. 'And there came unto me one of the seven angels... and he carried me away in the spirit to a great and high mountain, and showed me that great city, the holy Jerusalem, descending out of the heaven from God' (Revelation: 31:9,10).

She understood, the Holy City offered a threshold toward a greater dimension—a spiritual rapture in understanding and being with God.

It suggested, while on earth, we could continue on a journey toward this lofty destination. And to help us along the way, a growing and expanding capacity for God's light and strength was always available to us.

While contemplating the card's promise of peace and joy, she slipped into bed.

Early next morning, without giving much thought to her appearance, she automatically put on makeup, fixed her hair, and dressed in attractive clothes. On the subway ride to the studio, she recalled sitting in a screening room two days earlier with Jared and a few network executives. Together they viewed the completed tarot segment.

Although the small audience approved of the production, the real test would come from the public.

Without checking in with the receptionist, to keep her appointment with Jared, she took the elevator to the twenty-second floor.

Thinking this might be their final encounter she sucked in a breath of sadness.

She silently moaned, wishing they had met under different circumstances. But no amount of wishful thinking could change the truth.

As she knocked on his office door, determined to behave in a businesslike manner she forced herself to smile.

His voice rang out, "Come in."

She turned the knob and stepped inside.

Sitting behind his desk he asked, "Care for coffee or a pastry?"

She declined his offer, took a seat, and studied his face. As if engaged in a poker game, it didn't reveal a hint of emotion.

He told her, "You look great. I've noticed your new style. It's not only original it's very becoming."

Not sure of his sincerity she didn't respond to his compliment.

He asked, "Have you heard any feedback about the show?"

"Only from one of tarot's strongest critics, my mother. Before *Fact or Truth*'s credits finished scrolling on the TV screen, she called."

"And. What was her verdict?"

"She felt, while I didn't denounce or endorse tarot cards, I provided rich information supporting their original intent of providing a pathway to our Lord. When she praised me for a job well done, I reiterated tarot is only one guide to the Holy City. On their spiritual journeys, individuals have to choose their own paths."

"Did she agree?"

"In her opinion, tarot cards should be avoided at all costs."

"She's certainly entitled to her viewpoint."

"She still contends they have the potential to endanger a person's soul. I reminded her of a line from the segment, 'Tarot decks aren't good or bad, but people have the ability to either use them for lofty purposes or misuse them for malevolent ones.' Whether satisfied with my summation or not she's happy my assignment is complete."

He chuckled.

Cassandra asked, "What about the *Fact or Truth* audience?"

"In general the show received rave reviews and its ratings spiked to the top of the charts."

"Congratulations."

"Kudos to you. You're the person responsible for the segment's success."

"My job was only a small part of the production."

"Don't sell yourself short. Without your engaging personality, your alluring appearance, and your well phrased research materials, the production would've been a boring flop."

"I appreciate your kind words."

"They're not just my sentiments." He picked up a folder from his desk. "The network isn't going with Bev's idea. Instead, because of your contributions to *Fact or Truth* the execs decided to offer us a contract."

"I don't understand."

"Take a look for yourself." He handed her the folder. "General consensus is you're remarkable.

"Before the tarot-segment the top brass was about to dump my show, but you brought out a new side of me, an honest side. The execs see us as a winning team."

As she read the contract, her head began to spin. "I'm not interested. Tarot research encouraged me to reflect on my life and seek a higher purpose. I want to actualize my gratitude to God by giving to others." She placed the folder on his desk.

"Which means?"

"Meeting Sue helped me decide to do volunteer work. I recently joined a prison ministry. I've visited inmates, read the Bible with them, and shared inspirational true stories of people who made positive contributions to society during incarceration and after serving sentences. I realize this can be disheartening work, and I'm not cut out to do it full time, but it's inspired me to search out a new profession, one with meaning."

"Why can't you continue doing volunteer work while professionally working on our new series, a meaningful series?"

A shiver rippled through her. "I'm afraid I'll be tempted to forsake my ideals."

"Not going to happen. Remember, I thought I could corrupt you. Instead, you showed me the light."

He laughed, "Cassandra, I chose you for my experiment because you represented a genuinely moral person. Ironically, because you live your faith, you're reluctant to work with me. Maybe it's what I deserve. Maybe it's my punishment for my past indiscretions.

"Please don't bury your talents. You're too gifted to hide from the world. I'm the one who has taken without giving. Thanks to you, I too want to give back. And I'm convinced working with you is the best way to accomplish that goal."

Her puzzled expression led him to say, "Don't you see, our destiny is to be together and share with the world our gifts in exploring truth."

Confused, she just stared at him.

He placed his palms on his desk. "Okay. I'm willing to bow out of the *Fact or Truth* contract. I think I can convince the execs to have you as its sole anchor.

"With your ability to shed light on complex problems through understandable analogies, heck, you can start a new series."

"Keep your show. I don't want any part of it or anything more to do with show business."

As she rose to leave, he pushed back his chair, stood, and walked toward her.

Taking her by surprise, his arms encircled her waist. He lifted her, and twirled her around.

Her heart raced.

"Cassandra, don't you see we're in sync. We both want to find purpose through giving. We both want to live our faith. Granted, while volunteering and finding an altruistic job you'll be able to help a few folks. But I'm convinced, by having a national television audience you'll reach many more people."

He attempted to kiss her lips, but she turned her head to the side. He told her. "Joining together, connecting with our audience, and sharing truth can be like Isaac Newton illustrating that the combination of all colors creates white light.

"And by refracting light, or bending it through a prism different colors emerge. Please bend a little and give your life a chance to be decorated with vivid colors."

Resisting her passion, she squirmed out of his embrace.

He placed his hands on her shoulders. "I know I have to prove myself to you. I know I have to atone for my sins. I know I'll have to tread lightly and never again cast a shadow of deception between us.

"In time, I hope you might like me again and perhaps in the distant future love part of me."

She tried to block out his words by being pragmatic. "I could never forget what you did. I could never forget your repulsive bet."

"And I'm not asking you to, but don't let what I did hold you back. Don't you see by being anxious about the future you'll miss living in the present?"

She thought about her mother's incessant worrying robbing her of everyday happiness.

Jared kept talking. "Face it. You fear life. Yet, you've already passed the tests we all must face."

"And what might they be?"

"The same temptations the devil presented to Christ. I'm referring to the Gospel of Mathew.

"Firstly, 'Man doesn't live on bread alone but by every word that comes from the mouth of God' (Matthew: 4:4). Your quest in seeking God's truth was greater than money or the lure of material things.

"Second, 'Do not put your Lord your God to the test' (Matthew: 4:7). Throughout your tarot research, despite having your parents betray and reject you, while asking for guidance, you never doubted your faith. You didn't need God to rescue you to believe in Him.

"And thirdly, 'The Lord your God is the one to whom you must do homage, him alone you must serve' (Matthew: 4:10). Although you could see tarot's original beauty, you would never worship the cards. In short, you've always chosen to worship the Creator not any of His creations."

Cassandra felt guilty. Jared was giving her more praise than she was due. "If I was truly honest, despite you lacking any romantic interest in me, I would proclaim my romantic love for you."

He laughed long and deep. "I can't believe my ears. Cassandra I've been attracted to you as a gorgeous woman before we even met. My intentions were to seduce you, but once I fell in love with you, which was during our first face-to-face encounter, I chose not to give into my animal desires. I didn't want to exploit you in more ways than I already had. Moreover, from your behaviors, I thought you didn't view me as a potential lover."

She couldn't help but chuckle. "I always thought you could see right through me."

"Guess you're a better actress than you imagined."

"Once I found out about your experiment, I thought, no matter how painful, the only sensible thing to do was to stay far away from you."

He quoted from Father Henri J.M. Nouwen, "'Joy does not simply happen to us. We have to choose joy and keep choosing it every day.'"

The priest's words inspired her to confess, "I denied my happiness by not sharing the truth. You're my universe. I love you with all my heart and soul."

He embraced her. "You're my infinity and I'll love you forever."

He kissed her lips.

As she returned his passion, she felt a radiance lifting her to a new dimension.

From a heavenly realm, his earthly words reached her. "Let me be your cohost on the set and off."

She stepped away from him, moved toward the desk, flipped the contract pages, and with total confidence signed her name in several places.

He reached over her shoulder and signed his name under hers.

Inches from her face he said, "When I'm near you, I'm sure God's light is always aglow."

Cassandra turned to him. Caught in his magnetic stare she drew her body closer to his.

His arms enveloped her. "Are you ready to become Mrs. Jared Ashbel?"

She whispered, "I'm ready to share my love with you and its shining light with the entire world."

About E.B. Sullivan

E.B. Sullivan, PhD, a Kindle short story bestselling author, is a clinical psychologist who loves writing fictional tales. She draws inspiration from the amazing people she has met and the magnificent places she has visited. Her home, nestled in an enchanting California forest, is an idyllic setting to stir her imagination in penning creative stories, novellas, and novels.

Social Media Links:

Website: http://www.ebsullivan.com

Blog: http://www.ebsullivan.com/blog.html

Facebook: https://www.facebook.com/ebsullivan1

Twitter: http://www.twitter.com/ebsullivan1

Amazon Author Page: viewAuthor.at/EBSullivan

If you enjoyed this story, check out these other Solstice Publishing books by E.B. Sullivan:

Novels

Between The Vines

In her memoir, Lucia recounts poignant memories of life on a vineyard. She takes her first steps, experiences her first kiss, and learns primary lessons between the vines. Swept away by a passion to transform luscious grapes into superb wines, Lucia embarks on a romantic adventure laced with both tender and harsh realities. Cultivating grapes demands work, devotion, sacrifices, and expertise. Knowledge, timing and luck are necessary to make fine wines. Enlisting Old World philosophies and wisdom Lucia attempts to tackle personal and professional challenges.

http://bookgoodies.com/a/B01CO4611G

Alaska Awakening

A luxury Alaskan vacation turns into horror for three couples, who find themselves captives on a remote island in Prince William Sound for a thirty million dollar ransom. If their children don't pay, their chances for survival are slim. In the middle of despair, there is hope, forgiveness, and love—for their children, themselves, and each other.

http://bookgoodies.com/a/B00NOABMG4

Different Hearts

Beginning in 1840 Different Hearts parallels the lives of Sophia and Ezra.

Born with limited rights, Sophia struggles against societal norms. Conceived in rape Native American Ezra is an indentured-servant owned until his twenty-fifth birthday. The two meet and fall passionately in love. However, circumstances, prejudices, and personal guilt forbid their union. In the span of two decades, shared spiritual values transcend time and culture taking Sophia and Ezra on a journey from bondage to freedom.

https://bookgoodies.com/a/B0088L4ROS

Bloom Forever

While shopping at a secondhand store Dr. Sonia Wyland acquires Margaret's diary. Despite its flowery words, Sonia senses impending danger. She suspects infatuated Margaret is in the clutches of a psychopathic killer. Compelled to rescue her, Sonia travels to a quaint town where handsome William steals her heart. Despite her passionate feelings for him, she's relentless in pursuing Margaret. Is Sonia's analysis correct? Is Margaret in love with a psychopath? Is he planning to kill Margaret? Or, is Sonia avoiding intimacy by chasing a phantom?

https://bookgoodies.com/a/B00AY50AGA

Grandfathers' Bequest

Salvatore and Mariano make the mistake of stealing from the mafia. Realizing they will never be safe as long as they have the mob's cash, Salvatore flees New York for California, taking the ill-gotten gains with him, and burying them on a plot of land he purchased. Before the two men die, they bequeath the property to their grandchildren Elena and Luciano, but don't pass on the knowledge of where the treasure is hidden. In their search, Elena and Luciano discover much more than they bargained for.

http://bookgoodies.com/a/B00M7HP356

Dance Fantasies

A tragic night shatters Ava's dreams. Forty years later, she returns to her hometown searching for the man who stole her dance fantasies. During her quest, discoveries of hope, love, and romance abound.

http://bookgoodies.com/a/B010RABBXW

Short Stories

Island Homecoming

After years of pursuing a successful career, Anton plagued with guilt, bemoaning regrets, and bereft of faith, returns to the island of his youth. Once on familiar shores, he discovers most of the population has abandoned his homeland. In the process of accepting his island's fate, begging his father for forgiveness, and reconnecting with his past love, Anton faces spiritual challenges.

https://bookgoodies.com/a/B06XZV4HHX

War Kisses

Millie, a middle-aged spinster, witnesses WWII changing everything and everyone. Yet she's surprised when her school board lifts a marriage bar—banning married women from teaching—to alleviate a drastic teachers' shortage. In this new, liberated atmosphere, Millie is attracted to a dashing Air Force General, but fears becoming a victim of, hot, passionate, and fleeting war kisses.

https://bookgoodies.com/a/B06VY3W3SN

Balou Castle

Soon after arriving in Scotland, Cora wonders if the medieval castle she inherited from her mysterious Gran is a gift or a family curse. While renovating the structure, a frightful ghost haunts Cora's dreams and stalks her through gloomy spaces. Nightmares of her vile ex-husband intrude her thoughts. Between harrowing encounters, in order to keep her sanity, Cora savors the time she spends with a charming man who ignites her untapped passions.

http://bookgoodies.com/a/B01M35E1UB

Reality Pill

Sometime in the future, Dr. Kya Leeds creates a reality pill. Her first subject, Newman takes the experimental drug and sees his true past. In the process, he realizes greedy Dr. Uric will stop at nothing to obtain the pill's formula. To save Kya, Newman whisks her away from earth on a journey toward an uncharted universe.

http://bookgoodies.com/a/B01M0LL1MD

XOXO

Upon their first meeting, Vesti feels drawn to alien, Mina. Charmed by her unique beauty, her refreshing vibrancy, and her challenging ideas, he steps into her foreign world. She expands his perspectives by leading him to new horizons. Through their journeys, his dormant emotions awaken. With each encounter with Mina, Vesti gains a deeper understanding of true love. When her orb separates from his, the couple faces eternal separation. Forlorn Vesti decides to abandon his safe haven, encounter unknown risks, and ventures to an unstable environment in order to find his beloved, Mina.

http://bookgoodies.com/a/B01CEV0868

Reflecting Spirit

On the eve of traveling to Brazil Vicky overhears an intriguing legend about Mirana, a plain woman, who steps into a magic pool and becomes beautiful. During her vacation, guided by a handsome friar, Vicky explores Mirana's jungle. Despite his monastic ties, Vicky feels wildly attracted to this unattainable man.

http://bookgoodies.com/a/B01I2BS6GS

Visitor

Visitor" tells the tale of a retired schoolteacher who meets a surprise visitor while watching her four-year grandniece at a cabin hidden deep in the woods.

https://bookgoodies.com/a/B010693YY8

Spotlighting Crime

Allyson Barr is born in a prison, stalked by a psychopath, crisscrosses America meeting crime victims' families. In the process, Allyson learns valuable lessons especially regarding the importance of true love.

https://bookgoodies.com/a/B00E5NBNSG

Twinkling Lights

On her way to a dreaded work assignment Gladys finds a cell phone at an airport. In a quest to locate its owner, she encounters a fascinating man, examines her career path, and explores spiritual values.

http://bookgoodies.com/a/B01N2RG5GE

Christmas Escape

Lily hates Christmas. She has ugly memories of her alcoholic father spoiling festivities. She remembers him drunk, cursing, yelling, and hitting her brothers. As an adult, in order to escape Christmas, Lily vacations in warm places far from holiday fanfare. This year, while traveling from Chicago to Scottsdale, Arizona Lily meets a wounded ex-Marine. Despite his scars, she's immediately attracted to his seductive personality. She learns he is about to attend his sister's wedding alone. Lily takes a detour from her Christmas escape to be his date. At his family's ranch, Lily experiences a different side of Christmas. One filled with the magic of giving.

http://bookgoodies.com/a/B017TGEV9I

Christmas Guardian Angel

In their first encounter, Isabella becomes infatuated with Marc a handsome young man who makes fantastic potato chips. Fifteen years later while Isabella purchases a picturesque Victorian house she discovers Marc is the seller. His magnetism stirs her emotions and pulls her into his troubled world.

Soon Isabella realizes her new house, nestled deep in the woods, is haunted. By communicating with the house's spirit, she hopes to learn secrets, which can help Marc resolve his conflicted past and move him into the future. During the process, her love for him intensifies. As Christmas approaches, Isabella longs for Marc to return her affection.

http://bookgoodies.com/a/B009ONWL5Q

Christmas Between The Vines

Lucia wants a dog, but her family owns a vineyard and the puppy might ruin the vines.

http://bookgoodies.com/a/B019D7KHC6